Sludge Utopia

Sludge Utopia

Catherine Fatima

BOOK*HUG, TORONTO | 2018

FIRST EDITION

Cover image: *The Tower of Babel* by Pieter Bruegel the Elder. Public domain.
Inner cover photo by Amelia Ehrhardt and Alexandra Napier. Used with permission.

The production of this book was made possible through the generous assistance
of the Canada Council for the Arts and the Ontario Arts Council. BookThug also
acknowledges the support of the Government of Canada through the Canada
Book Fund and the Government of Ontario through the Ontario Book Publishing
Tax Credit and the Ontario Book Fund.

BookThug acknowledges the land on which it operates. For thousands of years it
has been the traditional land of the Huron-Wendat, the Seneca, and most recently,
the Mississaugas of the Credit River. Today, this meeting place is still the home to
many Indigenous people from across Turtle Island and we are grateful to have the
opportunity to work on this land.

LIBRARY AND ARCHIVES CANADA CATALOGUING IN PUBLICATION

Fatima, Catherine, 1990-, author
    Sludge utopia / Catherine Fatima.

Issued in print and electronic formats.
ISBN 978-1-77166-374-8 (softcover)
ISBN 978-1-77166-375-5 (HTML)
ISBN 978-1-77166-376-2 (PDF)
ISBN 978-1-77166-377-9 (Kindle)

    I. Title.

PS8611.A81S58 2018   C813'.6   C2018-900810-5   C2018-900811-3

PRINTED IN CANADA

Stimulation

MY DESIRES FORM A SYSTEM OF ETHICS, RIGHT? IF I DESIRE something, it is because I conceive of it as just—I desire what I think *should be*. When I demand what I desire, I put what I believe is right into action. Sometimes it does not go so well.

* * *

This has been a long, cold, sustained, slutty, and surprisingly even-keeled winter for me. I've been writing, keeping up with school. Things on paper are not difficult to formulate responses to; life is difficult to assess. I don't know—I feel good! I feel powerful lately, but not so much that it threatens to overwhelm me. Squash, still, each day. I often stay at home in the evenings, but sometimes I am tired from school, or I have work to do, or I cannot afford more. I haven't been falling behind on anything or feeling as though I'm on the precipice of doing so. Weight stable, skin fine, no illness. Annual review at work: positive. No drama. Few *challenges*, but each day I work hard.

This week, I presented a paper in Helena's class on Nancy's *L'Intrus* that was a joy to write. It was about health (avoidance of contamination), illness (the contaminated subject working in collusion with the harmful intruding substance), and *fitness*, the ability, necessary for life, to seamlessly incorporate foreign objects while identifying what within the self must be extruded to make its place. Writing is revealing, and I am in a place to reveal coherent things.

* * *

Helena invited me, with no provocation, to be her paid research assistant through the summer. Confusing. Nothing I've written to her formally is of particular quality. She likes the emails, the office visits, the missives. Until now, I'd only ever *wished* I could capitalize on them. It's a perfect opportunity to have fallen into.

Trying to think of some email to write her to ensure that I still *energize* her. Our focus in writing is writing itself: writing as a predictive act; different forms of it: "impressionistic" vs. "structural"; trust and seduction; the point of capture; how confusion or dislocation can be used to a writer's advantage; writing in silences, and how a reader can be provoked to complement a piece, fill in empty spaces.

For my own benefit, I want to figure out writing. I want to master the craft of language, play it like an instrument, deploy it to get what I want from a reader.

What brings me to a piece? What keeps me? Does theory excite me because it feels a bit incomplete, begging for my own supplement? I know I like to feel confused. I like it when the writer obscures something: I respond to this. I like when I feel the author has access to something that will be hidden from me until I've *worked*. Like Helena's. Someone, something, I just want to get to the bottom of.

This is difficult to achieve for oneself in undergrad. No one assumes you have access to anything.

* * *

Feeling odd in the world. Had a bit of a nightmare recently that I'd stopped being able to process progressive time, and every once in a while I have felt this way: out of place in time, like I can't quite remember what I did only yesterday. I suppose it's a feature of my lost/changing schedule. I've been feeling sleepy, a bit groundless, but fine.

On Friday, I went to a translation reading programmed by Blaise and Marianne. It was wonderful. Marianne was the clear star of the night, translated two psalms from, I think, three languages at once. When she spoke of her process, she was glowing. Detailed, witty, focused. I had never seen her present work before, but she was exceptional. It's so clear she'll have exactly the future she desires in academia. She was a force! And I was captured. I didn't feel I should try to compete with her, I was just excited to watch this woman present what she'd trained herself to be expert in.

She sat back down next to Julian. Memories of him: his theoretical boundness to an uncreative sort of piety. He was too committed to ideals—external, elusive—to construct proper, present narratives. The world wasn't enough: this was a limit. Me too. I went out in search of philosophy in distrust of myself, but also in distrust of others present to me, to have some sort of total truth revealed to me. Of course, I sought truths that I already recognized as true. This truth was still elsewhere, apart from me. Julian loved the Lord, and he loved the German Idealists. He loved the truth that would come if he only believed.

I need to consult others regarding matters to which I am too fearful to attest. I read to think: thank goodness someone else feels this way! Thank goodness someone recognizes this. Thank goodness someone else sees value in what I see value in. I seek authority to evade authority. I need explanations for the world because I think my own do not suffice.

* * *

What are some simple material things I would have in my ideal life?

—A nice apartment—not too big, but with a sun-
    room—shared with Ideal Boyfriend, yet unmet;
—in the light of the window of said sunroom, a
    medium-sized citrus tree that blossoms in the
    spring;
—a tabby cat, friendly but contained;
—this is it, I think.

* * *

I love this summer because I am always working and always moving and never have time to feel bad. Now working *another* day at the café, so I have five regular workdays per week between there and the library, plus off-shifts, plus the work for Helena. Depending on where I am, I may think: loneliness would be possible here, but I happen not to feel it. Seen some people around. Feel kindly toward everyone. I have had trouble sleeping. Despite how much I have been working, I have seen very little money.

The professional feels more important than the personal. No more taking relief shifts from work. None while I'm there.

None until I catch up with hours for Helena. It could mean very, very exciting things for me if I give her something she considers valuable! Time with family. My grandparents left for Portugal for the summer this evening. I'll miss them, I think. Not much feels narrative. Maybe because I'm not falling in love with anyone right now. Suits me better. I feel exhausted and good. Not stable. Not devoted to stability. Vulnerable and eager. Vulnerable and eager to fail. Or have a changed life. I'm really proud of all capacities in which I work for the university. And some friends I value more than it seems possible to. New ones each year. I guess it is compelling to be living.

* * *

I've had two seriously drunk nights over the past two weeks, but nothing feels shameful or burdening or lasting. On one, I slept with a stranger! A real, did-not-know-his-name stranger found at an after-party on the island offering free booze all afternoon and night, at which I also did a small amount of acid, invited to said after-party by one of the DJs, who had noticed my dancing. Regardless, slept with someone else—interrupted it, said, what am I doing! I have to leave and party with my friends! I remember his sense of duty in walking me to my bike. That was good. The other drunk night less notable. Julian was baptized yesterday. Not a joke. He invited his brother and parents to have them be witness to his baptism, which he orchestrated. He didn't tell me this; Blaise did. It upset me. Julian's burgeoning Christian faith, together with all these aspects of him, yearnings of his that I don't understand, are things I strictly do not want to know about. Slept with Paul a few evenings ago. This was nice. He said over email that he was daydreaming he'd have fewer bad Tinder dates if we just fucked again as easily as before. I agreed, but for a few days I felt no desire at all, then we had an afternoon pastry and an afternoon beer and fucked quickly, easily, hastily. It's always so fast with Paul. I enjoyed myself better than my qualitative assessment would suggest. I was seriously cheered up (for a half-hour). It was that his climax was so *pronounced*, so exaggerated, so spasmodic, so loud. I love a good, pronounced climax. Also recently had a long, long coffee with Helena. Talked about everything, family and men. She wants to publish our correspondence. I'm happy lately, I guess. Summer's good. As long as nausea's just a feeling and I don't set myself up to feel it again, summer's good.

* * *

Even when I try as stubbornly as possible to avoid a lovely life, it imposes itself upon me. Had sex with Paul again, and you know what? So nice. Seems like a stupid thing not to do. He is just absolutely not an insecure, shitty man. He doesn't come with all these complications. He looks great, touches well, and we speak evenly, honestly, in laughter. I don't want to kill him, but I like that during orgasm he behaves as though he is dying. Friendly. I told him Freida called me "the most transparent person" she knows (or one of), and he was like, really? One of the more opaque. Perhaps *the most* opaque. I tried to convince him otherwise. Wrote Helena a long email about ethics, vulnerability, and the self, and she *loves it*. Of course. Good finds me.

* * *

Trip away to NYC with Caroline; no personal writing; little alone time; no screens after certain hours. It was a lovely trip. We did lots. All introspection was shared outward. We: took bus; arrived to Penn Station; quick subway ride to accommodations at Bedford and Metropolitan; got coffee; walked around Brooklyn; took nap; ate Thai food; met a friend for a drink; spent some time at a midway, then by the water; good sleep in shared bed; to Manhattan for brunch at Shopsin's; walked around Little Italy, Chinatown, SoHo, in fancy shops; went to the New Museum; finally I suggested we part for a few hours; I bought books; read them; met her and another friend for a drink back in Brooklyn; we slept again, well (ate tacos from a truck on the sidewalk at some point); got coffee; long, long subway ride out to the Cloisters; the Cloisters is the most beautiful museum imaginable; the Unicorn Room; ate Venezuelan sandwiches at restaurant in far-far-north Harlem called Cachapas y Mas (I had a yoyo—mas); subway to PS1 for exhibition and party; big line for party and we excused ourselves, unimpressed; young women gave us wristbands; we get into everything for free; we didn't like the party but the Maria Lassnig exhibition feels to Caroline like the grace of God; crossed bridge on foot back to Brooklyn; browsed the Thing—I found an old Met postcard featuring one of the unicorn tapestries; we ate fresh foods from Polish grocer on steps of church; continued walking south until we found a bar uncool enough not to be crowded; Caroline and I read to each other, talked more, almost arguing for a moment (re: Ivan, Julian); slept well (actually, Caroline says she woke up this night—not me). Next morning, coffee on Havemeyer; subway down to Clinton Hill; Unnameable Books, more of it; walked down Vanderbilt to the Brooklyn Botanic Gardens; enrapturing; back up; tacos and fresh juice from trucks shared on front stoop; packed up; back to Manhattan; back home. Fin.

Caroline was never not speaking, and this at times alienated me. At other times, it soothed me. But so often I yearned for the quiet in my head. Until realizing, no, it's never quiet for long—by myself, it's always a-chatter with something, generally, that grieves me far more than whatever memory Caroline might be sharing. She seemed distractable. I learned she is more distractable *in general* than I had thought—it was always up to me to look to signs and guide us. Well, I always did it. Had I not, she would have, more slowly. I don't really feel the need to talk much at all past a certain threshold of speech. I sooner hum. She is a generous friend. It matters to her to be. I am much more parsimonious.

* * *

Love the limited time for thought this summer. Impoverished mind allows slightly less ailing soul, I think. I think! Went to a party of Ruby's after getting back into the city, and Helena was there. I was much too drunk. Long conversation about: being young, being quiet, being an ingenue, aging, choosing something else to be, being a mute, voicing oneself, living. Helena's a very sweet woman and I get along smoothly with her. Then I went to a second party and, with people from my teen years and some heavily sweetened punch there, I got *so wasted*. Fell asleep on the couch. Threw up, first time in a while. Arrived to this second party cogent but all at once forgot everything. I felt so wound up from the earlier portion of my night—I could have said *anything*. Quite a lot of binge-drinking this summer. Paul and I have both had to cancel on each other for sex dates, and no upsets at all? I struggle somewhat to understand the ease of this. Reading so little. Taking an intellectual dive. Not fascinated; unfettered.

Entirely happy with Paul's No-Cal Intimacy Substitute. I have no reason to flirt or date or seek anything elsewhere. It's so easy! It's really very nice! I like sex more all the time, and with strangers always less.

* * *

Another nice few hours with Helena. We've been exchanging lots of confessional juice about desire under power differentials. I haven't felt at all anxious about doing so. I'm so proud to be writing with Helena: I'm so proud to feel like I have something to offer the world besides myself in flesh. Personal writing is useful: we're not talking *around* anything. Fewer thoughts than ever reserved for journal recently as so many of them have been shared. Little feels private to me. Little even feels like it's better expressed in a private forum: things are best discussed. No new romantic feelings. No new feelings that I may be compromised. Perhaps the next person I fall in love with won't make me feel compromised at all. Imagine the kind of relationships I'd be able to form without looking to verify my intelligence and power through others, because I know I have them. Imagine not needing to be told I'm irresistible, that someone is doing anything wrong by being with me.

* * *

Always intend for painted nails to convey glamour, but they undermine me, each time, to indicate impatience.

Too much of a workhorse this summer. I'm losing much feeling. No leisure, no passion. Only work and rest. I feel *incredibly* anxious to leave the city again. Professionally, academically, yes, much is going on, but my personal life has staled. Intellectually, I feel stale, too, despite all the possible cues and calls. Need a reset button. Wish I had gotten closer to more strangers this summer: it's already chilling, winding down. Never stopping has its advantages in feeling less; it has its disadvantages, too. I haven't felt a hint of attraction to anyone new in months. More than a week without sleeping with Paul and I forget about it, too. I value my ability, better than ever, to have strong friendships with women, but I could use a bit of an influx of men, if only for the energy boost. I am getting old. Climbing rents in Toronto are a major psychic stress. Recurring dreams in the last couple of years: planes; islands; bodies of water; crashing planes; interiors of new buildings; inability to drive motor vehicles (paired with necessity of driving motor vehicles); women (more than men): last night (dreamt) fight with Caroline. I said something like, "Actually, I don't find the faith of others in any way fascinating," and she, pissed, walked off, in a sort of last-straw stance, announcing our friendship over. Conscious not so magical a place as the unconscious lately (I hate my [already-]aging body). Caroline and her partner's apartment will be torn down for development soon, too. Maurice's parents' house has been undergoing renovations this summer. Things are lost. Don't want to see it. I wonder which friends my age are now having love affairs with teenagers and how little I'd care. I have taken on a whole lot of continuous responsibility to prove to myself I'm not lazy. I am bored and want new things. I don't want to stop working for more than a moment because the luxury of stillness reminds me that it, too, requires cash. It's unbelievable the precarity that those better cared for have to endure, put up with, manage. They're able to lose what others just don't have.

It's odd to give so much of my writing away to Helena: something like a romantic relationship in its best stage, what I write for her seems each time to better match what she anticipates and desires, in part because I'm the one writing, and in part because I'm progressively better able to know what she wants. It's a bit depleting, though. Without her interpolation,

I'm sure I'd be producing something else. Next summer: I will write something for myself, and I will do it without working twenty other jobs.

* * *

At a very, very good party Ivan hosted last weekend, I met Helena's brother, Oreste. We got along well. He's a comedian. He wrote to say it was great to meet, and Helena, having gotten wind of it, asked, too, if I'd like to come see him perform tomorrow night. Of course, I must. And for the first time in some time, I'm terrified. He seems collected, witty, kind, worthwhile.

I've been loving this summer, but I cannot keep up.

* * *

Spent the night with Oreste after his show. I barely even have language for this. It was just—it was perfect. I am so excited by him. I love the way he speaks and I love what he says and I love the symmetry in our speech and I feel very nervous without feeling self-conscious, certainly never being made to feel so, and he doesn't seem to possess meanness at all. Oreste is very smart and very witty but never pretentious and never snide. Always attentive. Always attentive. Never too fumbly (I am more so than him—it is certain). I am frightened and lucky. OK. I assumed Helena had invited me to see Oreste as a sort of setup, and I assumed it was due to communication that the two of them had shared. I was a bit correct. Helena later told me that this constituted "thirty per cent" of her intention. And Oreste, for his part, seemed to be caught off guard by this conclusion when I brought it up to him after his set. He seemed worried about my professional relationship to Helena, and then I felt *very* embarrassed and *very* foolish to have wrongfully assumed that Oreste might have told Helena he was interested in me. After this misunderstanding, I thought he was merely attempting to shield me from hurt and embarrassment for a few minutes while we both finished our drinks. He offered to walk me to my bike, and we spoke nervously about nothing for a few more minutes, and then I hugged him goodbye. He reached for my arm, and I gave him one single, apprehensive kiss—pulling right back—but, as I realized he *wanted* this, I sprung forward for another, and that one *lasted*. See: I don't even know how to recount this kiss to sufficiently convey how this kiss felt or what was done to me by this kiss. It was vexing. Just, I don't know, each sensation perfectly balanced; everything hit just the right note; we got in so close to each other; it lasted for a few minutes. A hard smack in the face. The thought of walking twenty-plus minutes to either of our apartments wasn't pleasant to face: I biked and he took a taxi. And then, at mine, no disappointments. He's so great! Love kissing him. Incredible stamina. Great grip, lots of pinning down, lots of everything. It was too much! It was unlike any first time I've had with anyone, I think—I think? Pretty sure. I just couldn't believe it and could not have asked for more. Conversation in the morning (and second fuck): great. He's very polite, very respectful, and I'm anxious not to say things that are objectionable, but that's the worst it gets, I guess.

* * *

Oreste makes me feel eerily sure of wanting to be near Oreste. Not even *wanting*—a feeling of, what else? What other decision would I make? Finally, I'm not choosing between men in a series of qualifying binaries—yes, I'm stimulated but not turned on, I'm turned on but terrorized, I'm calmed but not

18

enthralled. I don't know. He inspires all of these good feelings in me, satisfies everything he needs while never frightening me or making me feel inadequate. I feel "natural" with him, exactly myself, able to articulate things exactly how I'd like, never either venerated or ignored, and I'm so *turned on* by him. Finally, I can look to someone for everything—and such a circumstance makes my desires easier to control. I have no compulsions toward him, no feeling of mania. He says I seem incredibly comfortable with myself, in myself. With him, I am. I'm managing not to feel frightened absolutely to death of when something disrupts this. I just cannot envision not wanting to be with him. He has surpassed so many expectations. He's wonderful! Perhaps he's no more wonderful than I am and, finally, we've found the other with whom we're properly compatible. It does feel like what I imagine others have meant by *compatibility* all this time. I met him eight days ago. We've spent the night together *twice*. All the same. Why would I want to stop? No other men in sight. Just none. I don't feel nostalgic and I don't feel the urge to "test" myself before others. This is the fucking best.

I'm at a loss for even being able to properly describe how I feel about Oreste to friends. Infatuated? Well—not simply. The immediate ease of being with him resembles no previous involvement. And he doesn't leave this aching impression behind upon me. I'm not worried. How has this circumstance been so kind?

* * *

MY LORD, WHAT LUCK TO BE IN SUCH A BLISSFUL FEELING.

It's like I'm on only the good parts of Cipralex. Had beers

with Caroline last night and she could tell, too. Things in my head are very sunny. What do Oreste and I even say to each other? I never remember. I love to be touched by him. Feels perfect. Any impression he makes upon me is the right one. So much warmth. Into it.

* * *

Blaise says, in life there are two things: learning new words and learning new ways to fuck (my interpretation: new ways to enjoy, new desires to discover that one has, or has had all along). Say, this is true. Then, I think, it is very good to live.

What a warm blanket I've had draped over me for days. I feel secure and peaceful, constantly. I don't see only Oreste. I see lots of lovely friends in lovely life. Summer is drawing quickly to a close! Final Monday shift at the library tomorrow, three shifts left at the café—then *one week off*—my Lord! And then: another year of classes begins.

* * *

Even my digestion has improved. I don't understand what happens when I feel well. Keep living? Like this? My God. I think more when I'm upset. And those thoughts speed time's passage. Days enjoyed are so slow. Ivan's party was two and a half weeks ago? This is possible? These weeks, unequivocally wonderful, have been, I fucking swear, the longest of my life.

Still scary, though, insofar as desire for Oreste leads me to believe that I must be less to him than he is to me, not due to mistreatment on his part, but simply due to this feeling that the entirety of my being is a more minimal thing than my interest in him. And he must know, right? He is working to supplement me, so what I feel for him is gratitude for this. He should tire of me, I'm sure, just as I do when I am larger to others than they are to me.

* * *

Feeling a little apprehensive today. You know what is annoying about myself? This fucking precious optimism all the goddamned time. For a few weeks, I have either been waking early to go to work or waking with Oreste, and today I did neither. This allowed me to enter a quiet space of contemplation, which is safe for only so long.

I'm sure I feel this way often, but I just don't think my own thoughts are valuable lately. I feel like my mind is lazy and not attuned to all it once was. The pleasure of working so much, constantly being available to serve others in this underconsidered way, is alleviating to stress, but then I return to myself and, only after so long, thought improves, but I *feel* worse. So. I don't know. I don't know where the compromise is.

Two days ago, went to visit Max on the island after work (he is there for one week), ran into friends, and suddenly it was an arrangement totally of another kind, with hours spent drifting on a small boat in smiling company, and a quiet barbecue at a house on Ward's. The perfect summer afternoon and evening, truly.

I should feel a *bit* inadequate, right? That just means it matters to me. This lovely neutral place where I feel neither inadequate nor superior: well, that's just how I feel when I'm actually *with* him.

* * *

On the street today, some man handed me a business-card-sized advert for God, and is this really in the Bible? It's sort of good:

GOD: If there is anything separating me from you, please take it.

Reminds me otherwise: YOU ARE LOVED/YOU ARE LOVED/ MY FRIEND/YOU ARE LOVED/BY JESUS/GOD IS LOVE. Poetry.

Still, Oreste has not decided to leave me. What luck. Spending time with him is exquisite. There are so few blockages. I always feel good around him, and I never feel like it takes much effort. He says of me (when I want, but he is too tired, to fuck in the morning), you're so energetic! But I don't feel that way. Before him, I don't feel like I must drum up any energy at all; I always feel exactly prepared for the particular demands of being with this person. And further still, he gives me whatever energy I need. It never feels like surfeit; it's never too much. I have exactly what I need before him, and it doesn't leave too much residue behind. I don't feel I much need God's love.

God, it's so strange not to drink too much and not to say too much and not to sleep around and not to sabotage. A picture of control without restraint. Who knew I could display it. It's just so fucking easy.

Worked final day at the café yesterday. Though I enjoyed my summer there, it didn't feel like much to have it end. I suppose that means I'm not anxious for what is next.

Depression

On the evenings I enjoy most, I wish I could masturbate without porn, which I find tacky and ugly.

* * *

I'm finally feeling a bit of anxiety regarding Oreste, with whom I suppose I couldn't possibly sit in a bed of flowers forever. It's still good, but it lacks the remarkable ease with which it began. I fear that without the same explosiveness, I might become boring to him. How soon can such a thing happen? We only fucked in the morning the first couple of nights we spent together. I find it difficult not to reveal my fear of growing boring, adding to the threat. He'll see that I'm not as comfortable with myself as he thought.

"Stimulating": intellectual/sexual: different meanings: the first beginning an active process of thought, continuous past that beginning; the other just allowing/facilitating an experience of pleasure.

All good things coming. Um. Maybe just not as many times per night as before—

* * *

What do I write privately when I've already shared everything with Oreste and Helena? I have no reason to feel nerves with Oreste because, on one occasion, he left my apartment to do stand-up at one in the morning. Hard to get used to the sort of involvement where this wouldn't signal a renunciation.

Had some wine in the park with Marianne. She slept with Julian this summer (post-baptism, naturally), and he told her, first, that he'd slept with a prostitute earlier that day and, second, that he "wished [her] mind was like [her] vagina." She said he couldn't stay hard. And that she picked him up as he was reading the Bible alone at a dad-jazz bar. Thanks to the Lord that I am detached.

Oreste joked that if I wanted to do a stand-up set, he could certainly get me one. Sort of made me desire it. I don't think I'd be able to come up with a single joke that didn't involve sex. At least laterally. I don't think one should do stand-up if a man she is sleeping with offers to facilitate this. Specifically not if he is joking himself.

Left Toronto briefly. Have really been having the slowest, calmest, most wonderful time in Montreal. Final weekend of summer going splendidly. Meditating on what I get so nervous about re: Oreste, fearing that I will seem or become boring. It's so absurd. First meeting, he admired my slowness. It's foolish that I might have behaved initially with such ease, and now, learning to feel anxiety again, I compromise this. Return. There's no reason not to feel this ease. There's nothing I must rush to display, nor anything I must rush to cover up. He's with you on purpose. Feel fine.

* * *

Oreste is not forcing me to do comedy and I cannot bring myself to admit that I *would like to.*

Thought when secretly devising stand-up set that, OK, the primary ethical conundrum of a woman's sexual life is how to take the reality of a world that does not work in her favour—a world of desire that subjugates her—and learn to get off on this, while behaving in a manner that is ethical such that, perhaps, you might change the landscape of sexual desire for women who come up after you. You must allow for a better future while getting off on its present. Just needs a punchline.

Reading *Dora* in a café. OK, in the midst of Dora's father's failings, she feels attracted to his friend, and fantasizes, on occasion, that they will wed. Despite this, she, recognizing him as a seducer, pushes him away to save herself from this attraction. What Freud tells Dora will not change her life. It's lovely for Freud to have invented for himself a fantasy of a time where catharsis might be enough. Now we must live with hyper-attended knowledge of our neuroses—choosing which to nourish and which to starve, and how, exactly, to indulge those neuroses we should. There is so much objectionable content in *Dora* (*so much*), but perhaps the worst of it is that Freud attests—maybe even in earnest—that if Dora hadn't left treatment just on the brink of his simple breakthrough, she might have been "cured" of her hysteria. She would be cured of her hysteria because her doctor could tell her of the preciousness of her love for this irresponsible seducer—so she could know very well: I wish to put in place this man I can fuck for a father whose attentions left me? How far from this knowledge might Dora have actually been? Upon such a realization comes the hard work: one must live, still, an entire life dealing with the disappointments and difficulties upon which such an unpleasant fantasy could be founded in the first place.

On giving oneself up and what it looks like: I feel prohibited from letting Oreste know that I am anxious for contact from him, or how I relish it, or that I wish our contact between seeing each other could be of slightly stronger sexual/emotional content, because I feel like this would relinquish control of myself to him in a way that is, chiefly? Not attractive. I don't think it would turn him on to play with this thing I give him: oh, immediately as I hear from you, I feel good; otherwise, I feel terrible! He has other business to attend to sometimes, and this sort of behaviour is demented. I have things to attend to, too. I'm often slow with him. Is this pacing resistance? Is Freud correct in saying that all emotion is experienced, like orgasm, as continuous buildup of tension to a point of release? I'd prefer not.

How about the injunction that we all *should* sublimate—be better Freudians—in order to keep our desires in frisson, building pressure to burst forth from contained spaces, rather than to release prematurely and thus relinquish—or even to simply squander—our emotions? What of that I think it sucks.

Hold the phone, I just realized for-sure for-sure that it's really fucking tough not to behave exactly as you're used to behaving all the fucking time (I don't get exactly the attention I want from Oreste; I want to throw the relationship, and him, under a fucking cargo van).

"It's just enough" as (always) code for: "It could really be a bit more."

Basically, with love, I want to think nothing. I just want to live in the fragrance of it. And never see Oreste again and come home and fuck the shit out of Paul.

* * *

First thing: Oreste is not Julian, nor Max, nor anyone or anything else. Major difficulties with projection cause me to replicate each old lover as a new one, put them beside each other so they resemble one another, interpret actions of *some* variety so that all motives are the same. But this is not true. It's not even true that I'm attracted, always, to the same sort of man, just as it's not true that they're all bound to treat me the same way unless I invite them to do so. Oreste is not the same. Oreste is concerned with ethics, and not terribly good at communicating things of a delicate nature. God, I like Oreste.

Was not incorrect to notice a pullback on his behalf. Last night, he told me that a friend of his is drafting up papers for a visa so that he may move to Los Angeles this fall. Oh, OK. This was brought up following Oreste's having forgotten, apparently, the morning he mentioned wanting to find an apartment here in October, and maybe a secondary job outside comedy to stabilize his days. He said of this, he *would* like to settle, but Toronto is not the city.

We had this conversation at a bar, not terribly close to either of our beds, and I was *certain* we were meeting so I could be told he didn't want to see me any longer. But apart from discussing his uncertainty about Toronto, we didn't really discuss things between us at all—or we did, a few things, playfully and easily. He said he was happy for the change in scenery, feels like he barely knows me in public. I told him, too, about feeling specifically compromised by only ever having him to *my* apartment, that he has the opportunity to view all these extensions of me, that I feel comparatively so much on display. He seemed intrigued and hadn't even considered this—"I can send you pictures of my old apartment, if you'd like."

* * *

Safety in lost objects: they certainly can't deprive you of anything *more*. Slightly sick with unknowing this autumn. It's insane to me how long spaces in between seeing Oreste actually feel. Unpunctuated. It's strange to even feel the desire that wants a cock, specifically, inside. I frequently want a kiss, a little affection, but not to be penetrated, which sometimes quickly annoys. Not lately! My Lord. I so desire penetration. Specifically. From one.

Binge-drank for the first time in a while, again, on Thursday, for my course union's "bonding" drinks. I have such an urge to economize when it comes to drinks free of cost. Started drinking earlier than anyone else alone with Maurice. Confided in him my sadness regarding the situation with Oreste, realized aloud: no, I really *don't* have any idea where things go from here, how things are, even, at present.

Interlude: it is crazy how much better masturbation has been lately. I am delivering some unnatural orgasms to myself. Get so excited—so excited!—by smiles and the touching of faces. I daydream about Oreste to serious excess. My best hopes are to turn him on even a fraction as much. I can't even tell him this stuff because this isn't the sort of dialogue we carry on. It isn't the sort of dialogue he likes to carry on. I just have to be impossibly turned on, so often, completely alone. It's a lot to carry. So I'm looking real fucking forward to when Oreste is back in my GD apartment so I can put what I can't speak into practice.

I mean: identity seems to make a case for itself when it's *so hard* to change one's behaviour, it's *so impossible* not to behave in exactly the same ways forever. (A new prof, a young and attractive man, who seems, too, to be a little nervous and on somewhat poor footing, is already giving me undue attention—I am, despite my better knowledge, delighting in it.) Instincts to suppress writing double entendres to my professors must be cultivated, because the opposite instincts come more naturally. Each year, all the same, I am doomed to be myself.

* * *

So few thoughts produce when I can't convince myself of their privacy. Yet privacy can be between two. The thoughts that produce for Helena: in our own private discourse (even if produced in some writing chamber for their eventual release into the world). She's not teaching me this semester, but I still write for her. I trust her: I trust her to gracefully receive all I should give her. There are no deaf ears. Impediment to writing or speaking: when you don't know where your words will go or under what circumstances they will be welcomed. Too long without satisfactory affirmation, and the lines of communication close. You have privacy not with the object, but from it. This, I imagine, is the end of any relationship.

I find it easier to direct my thoughts to school, direct my thoughts to *anything*, if I imagine that Oreste and I might separate completely. Then I will not have privacy *with* any love object and I will return to stability once again. The nice parts—not the hateful parts—of identity will return to me. Just those parts of identity that tell me I have a history to think about, that I am some accumulation of experience, so I shouldn't ever be bored with myself. That part of identity that can finally shelve away the most recent love affair with all previous love affairs as a new but discarded contribution to my former life.

Spent almost five hours at Helena's house on Sunday, talking about femininity and humanity and identity and power. In her thrall, I'm always seeking to make myself as similar to her as she seems to want me to be, as we are both women who've had affairs. She speaks through—and assumes me to have shared—a preternatural sense of control over lovers. I really *don't* believe I share this. I hardly ever have any idea what I'm doing. Tried not to address Oreste directly. Went to see him do a set this same night; left early, didn't invite him over, could have broken up with him right then and there were the goodbye kiss not, as always, so good. Now he's on tour for a week. And soon, another. I don't want us to write or fill the physical absence with verbal presence because such a presence is a strong one that, for me, permeates everything.

Helena says all her relationships have been profoundly passionate; she barely has any of the slighter ones. It *is* much more affirming to date hyperverbal men who always have something to share.

Paul wrote a nice story that's getting good circulation on the internet, but I think it's socially irresponsible to over-romanticize disaffection. To me there's an injunction not to dwell there, and to pretend, instead, that it doesn't exist.

* * *

Really a shame that infatuation is far too pleasurable to convincingly renounce. Oreste and I clarified (at—smart for me but idiotically for him—*my* behest) that we won't spend time together anymore. Pretty very sad about the most enjoyable three weeks of my life, but there are always discrete periods. So much late-onset discomfort. Never more sad than when feeling so much more comfortable communicating with exes than with present lovers. Well. More sad now. Otherwise.

Max told me a few nights ago, perhaps through a slip of the tongue, that he would marry me. Hypothetically, I think. I didn't ask! It's a strange thing to be told by someone you had never even comfortably called a boyfriend. How he cherishes me when I do not date him. Days ago I was still seeing Oreste, technically, told Max so, he seemed unsurprised. Oreste and I are a bit alike, he thinks. I don't really think I am so similar to Oreste. I remember how sad I was when Max broke up with me, four years ago. Quietly, unrelentingly sad, with no resentment: nothing to hold but my experience of loss. And that passed. Because all wounds that one does not pry apart heal. And then you're better, different. I don't want to marry Max and I tell him so even though I had, for all intents and purposes, a perfect night.

Infatuation is awful. Arrive whole, glowing, proud—leave soft and mushy and terrible. Then reform again, knowing just what will happen.

Feel bad. I'm anxious about how bad, *cumulatively*, I'm likely to feel this fall and winter. The aim-inhibition involved in *not* telling Oreste that we should have one final parting fuck is obscene. I suppose *one* wouldn't do much. Postpone lack of pleasure. Give me just one hit before slower weeks. I know it would do nothing. Probably wouldn't even feel right to him.

How could someone who fucks like Oreste experience such prohibitions. Life: sucks. Nothing even *starts*.

Celibacy is good, I guess. Plenty of good things come to celibate people.

Maybe the *real* reason I sleep so fucking much is to prove wrong the men who call me "energetic," but as the sleep is private to me, this is not a good strategy.

OK, CATHERINE. JUST BECAUSE FREUD SUGGESTED AIM-INHIBITION SHOULD BE WORN AS LINGERIE DOESN'T MEAN YOU'RE BEHOLDEN TO THIS. EVERY TIME YOU THINK OF DOING SOMETHING STUPID JUST GO AND PLAY SQUASH INSTEAD. NO ONE IS EVER FORCING YOU TO BE A FUCKING IDIOT.

I asked because I have bad impulse control but also because if he says yes I really fucking want it. (Because I have bad impulse control and because I am a fucking idiot.)

* * *

Oreste and I fucked our final time. We almost did not speak at all, but there were moments and images ready to stick in my head for daydreaming afterward. He had exactly the energy I wanted: fierce, forceful, intense. It's strange: the way Oreste is good in bed, it's almost as though there's no room for me—he's firm, so much in control of it: the pace, the position. There's no blank time, no moments of indecision, no talking, no pausing, just all at once I'm being fucked a new way or at a new speed, or someone's genitals are in the mouth of the other. I was fucking so instantly giddy that barely a minute after his arrival into my house were we panting, completely undressed, he's already thrusting into me. I feel as though I am ravaged, and I *want* to feel so; it turns me on insanely. All the same I can't ignore how invulnerable this sort of sexual behaviour makes someone: to be in control, he must be *completely* in control.

I wonder when I will get over porn on the basis that porn that looks like the sex I *want* to have simply doesn't, and surely could not ever, exist. Oreste and I fucking could not be caught on camera.

Neither of us slept well. Slept touching—not at first, but then consistently. Had to be up early for work. We both showered and dressed. The mood was not solemn, but it was scarce. When he asked me, even, how my week had been, I hardly felt prepared to answer, and only barely did. Volleyed the question back at him, same sort of response. Out most nights. Many shows.

Didn't feel anxious—sort of unburdened and slow, like the beginning. The few words I spoke were not slurred or self-monitored. He made some comment, as I was putting on my shoes, about how I was "always running around." I told him, like the various times he's commented on my *energetic nature*, it's not *really* a compliment to call me energetic, because I don't feel this way about myself. It's so little of me—something I have a tenuous hold over that it distresses me to lose. I said, it shouldn't be this decisive or attractive factor about someone, something they struggle so much to maintain. I don't know that he understood. It's strange to speak one's impressions of another at all. I don't think I do this with new people, tell them, you're this, you're this, you're this. How am I supposed to know what they are! Early impressions are cloudy. I can't distinguish between the different parts that make a person up. And I don't possess this instinct to *tell someone about themselves.*

We both said the night was nice and kissed in short pecks. Neither of us said goodbye forever, because neither of us could bring ourselves to do so. Nevertheless, it had already been said—we were simply fulfilling the closing terms of our agreement. We had texted each day, about almost-later-fucking, until it happened, but there has been no contact since (two nights ago). That's OK. I mostly feel good. I mostly just drift off into fantasies of the quickness of our fuck's beginning, or the strength of his hands.

I am alone, again.

* * *

I had a very nervy, interior, hyperenergetic but detached weekend. I feel a mild hysteria. Can't stop thinking about Oreste, and Helena, too. How I've looked lately to either of them. The way Oreste saw me never satisfied me: of course I should be eager to seek recognition instead from Helena, as what she sees in me so perfectly corresponds to what I'd *like* to have seen: a strong, complicated, knowing woman who is unstoppably irresistible, always compelling in her thoughts, and in control. Any comment Oreste might make about me seemed minimizing, to the exception of something else. The comments were fixing: I lived such a way, was such a way: "free," "confident," "energetic." I am only these ways as much as I am their opposites. I want to be understood one way or another, I just don't want someone to vocalize to me that they've chosen *which*.

Too many Dworkian metaphors at work in heterosexual couplings: the man, desiring, should want to get to the bottom of something, and the woman should want to be bored into; the man should want to *be* incorporated, and the woman should want to incorporate.

Why should vulnerability seem like an absurd thing to allow oneself? Because it *is*. To seek affirmation from a person who must recognize in you something you desire to be seen in yourself, having *not known you*—that is nonsense. You won't get what you want. You will either suffer disappointment (what they see in you fails totally to meet the fantasy of what you want to have seen in yourself) or, otherwise, you'll be surprised (what they see in you won't *match* what you'd wished to have seen, it will surpass it). It will be a reading for which you are not prepared, and this very lack of preparedness will facilitate a rupture in the Freudian sense—we can only *really* be struck by what we don't see coming.

* * *

Yesterday evening, amid fantasies, I told Oreste we should sleep together once more before he leaves Toronto, though I don't know when this will be. He said, "Catherine, I don't know. This makes me sad ultimately." I said, sure, it makes me sad, too, but at least not during. He said, yes, but after. I said, what difference does it make, I'm already sad. He said, it obviously won't make anything better. I said, you're right. He said nothing else. I didn't say, as I nearly did, that he could not imagine how I wished to delay having to meet and flirt with and kiss and fuck someone *new*, the fucking grim realities of the next person I meet who will not hold me like he does, with whom it will not be as it was. I did not tell him that after our first kiss, I am fucking *spoiled* for first kisses. I didn't tell him, because I don't want to manipulate, and because I don't feel I had an equivalent effect on him at all, and I feel pathetic.

There are some things I know and, with each romantic failure or loss, must remember:

—IT ENDS. Things feel bad if you want them and they end. *You should feel bad.* If you are feeling bad, the right thing is happening. If you are feeling compensatorily powerful or sped or denying, the wrong thing is happening, and you are stunting yourself. As with quitting smoking, each time you indulge, you only lengthen your withdrawal time. Loss feels horrible. You can fool yourself into rushing through it, but it will still feel deeply and magnetically horrible until some very surprising day when you forget to think about it, and such a day will only be postponed by fucking them again, or even telling them that you want to fuck again, which is a virtual version of the same thing. You will not be made to feel good by courting your own failure through a lost relation. There is no counter-argument to this. There is only bad impulse control.

—Parting will obsess you with equivalence: the stubborn insistence that your desire either was or could not have been equal to that of your partner. Such a thing cannot be quantified and, were it possible: even total equivalence of feeling will not save you from your loss. Is it embarrassing to think that you did not do to another what they did to you? Certainly. Are seduction, affection, intimacy not made up largely of embarrassments? They *are* largely made up of embarrassments. Save yourself the experience of thinking about it.

—If you feel like this love has ruined you for other loves, there is little purpose to indulging further dalliances for the sake of distraction. Remember that, as the last time, the next time you fall for someone will be by surprise: it will not be deniable, and you'll know desire is coming.

* * *

I did a heavy dosage of mushrooms with Ivan last night, but I believe my newer, optimistic lease on life will be fleeting until I put it into practice. It is clear to me that avoiding sex and relationships is the best tactic if I am feeling a great deal of loneliness, confusion, and anxiety. Also. Came to terms with being a verbally and emotionally demanding woman, with a primally annoying soul.

Many other thoughts, like: I feel nostalgia for earlier in life, when I was closer to an amplified, hyperactive verbal state more often. I was unstable, but in some ways had access to a greater portion of my mind's faculties. Now I have stable, responsible attention and I've lost much of the freedom of being young.

Still, the major conclusion I came to with these drugs is that no one has been kidding about these drugs. They are the real deal.

Every man I date just feels like the next wild animal released to eat the smaller one (Oreste devours who preceded him, but now *he* is the one loose).

* * *

OK, OK, I am going to do some work after copying what I wrote on my cellphone's memo app on Saturday night on the drugs (retaining initial placement of line breaks and capitalization):

This mental activity feels really good!
But sad
Mostly I feel sad about Julian, with whom I was the most 16 years old, because I was actually that age
And a lot of the time it felt like this
Hugely stimulated
And I would share the weirdest shit, and always have it matched with the good, right, weird shit
I need someone with the most supportive and surprising mental activity
Who makes me feel at home, no matter what
Why is this so hard to find?
Look it's very sad that no one should be fucking rushing to comply with my enormous verbo-emotional demands
They are also DICK DEMANDS
they are ultimately simple and exactly right for me
I DO WANT WHAT I WANT
EMOTIONAL TAUTOLOGY IS REAL
it's also not so bad.

No one will ever be able to take away from me that I have dated some of the best looking men in Toronto

Like I feel I wouldn't turn away anyone who met my emotional demands exactly.
So, OK, why would anyone else, I guess I fail in

many ways to meet the emotional demands of people.
Or, OK, in not drugs life we're not all so busy making emotional demands

I want the shit?!
Life is sad. Someone put their shit here, please.
In NOT TEEN LIFE we're not all so busy I was great as a teenager at making adult teens fall in love with me how do I now as an adult make adult adults fall also in love with me while feeling just as safe as the adult teens now this is a hugely difficult question.
The problem of living has really been that I am the only one who finds myself this funny.

Going to give my therapist a real talking-to for not coming to a few of these conclusions first.

* * *

Things are not very good. They have not been very good in some time. I sleep constantly. I throw all my time away. I do not take school seriously. I don't see friends much. I am slobbish. I primarily eat takeout food. I was physically sick for a time and too heavily fixated upon it. I do not possess the requisite attention for life. I am elsewhere. I am *no*where. I am vacant and bereft. I have felt neither very stimulated nor comforted at school, getting few new surprises. *No* new surprises. Everything is stale. I am not setting expectations for myself to meet. But I'm so *tired* all the time, OK?! Life does not seem exciting. Books don't seem exciting. My insights don't seem exciting. I don't launder my sheets often enough. I'm gaining weight. I feel weak. I play a bit of squash but not enough. My world feels small and unlikely to expand.

This period of life that I'm in—I don't know how to not be in it. I don't understand how else I so recently lived. I don't understand so recently being gratified by my thoughts, by myself. The only energy I possess is the nervous sort. I feel nauseous and unhappy. I don't know how to fix it. I can't do anything. I feel sick. I don't know what to do.

I feel so, so lonely. I am worried about my future. I feel I'm failing my future. I feel totally uncertain about the future I'm bound to have. I can't write. I am fucking up my life. I am delaying my life. Even my delayed life will not be the one I want. At least I look young. In the spring I'll be twenty-five. It will not have gotten warm yet, and there I'll be, barely closer to graduating from college, single, always, and twenty-five. No one older than me would consider this old. But these are people who have graduated from college.

* * *

I think I spent four or five of the last twelve months this year continuously satisfied, stimulated, healthy, and happy, which—as far as years? Pretty competitive.

* * *

Of the lovers who bore into us most skilfully: that we recognize in them something we shamefully expect of ourselves, that we are drawn to and want to cleanse them of (e.g., they are sociopathic, serially seductive, hyperverbal with no proper place to put it and, God forbid, *honest* about all these personal failings).

* * *

So, lately:

—Time with Freida, editing in her studio, which has mostly been an excuse to spend time together;

—Slept, once, with Oreste again. It was a terrific evening. Ran into each other at a show and kissed hello continuously. I hadn't seen him in over a month, mostly he had been on tour, and it was so *relieving*. Lovely to be caught in this heat of public passion: chatting, running around from one room to another, hands touching, kissing lots, holding each other, all night. It was as if the whole week hadn't been awful. So, he came over; we rode in a taxi together. He is moving away soon, permanently. He doesn't like it here, and we haven't spoken since the evening.

—Ivan tells me I shouldn't be so conservative with myself where it concerns Oreste, but Ivan is fucking wrong.

—Helena started to email again. I'll still be doing a hint of work for her. Hardly anything. We had a meeting at her house last Friday afternoon and it was a treat. It occurred to me she might have handed me down her only slightly worn copy of *Either/Or* in order to torture me (you see—Oreste read from it the night Helena brought me to see him do comedy), but: this is crazy. This is not a reasonable thing to think.

Resigned myself to the pretty unavoidable circumstance of having sacrificed this semester for myself academically. You cannot fail your future by taking too long. There is no deadline for life.

I have no one to ask: can't I just feel good enough for the both of us?

The afternoon after my last night with Oreste, Max asked if I wanted to have lunch. I biked down to Parkdale, we had Tibetan food. Max is in touch with the things one should be in touch with. He asked about Oreste, and I told him: it "ended" soon after he and I last hung out, but only insofar as it went from a thing with some accountability to a thing with none, but *now* it has ended, really, because he's moving, for months. He told me about someone new he had been dating, but that it seems to have ended, too. He says she's my age, but not like me. I ask, what does that mean, what sort of way am I that someone can be unlike? He says: calm, introverted. I know I'm trying to get over the investment in being affirmed by what others might see in me, but it makes me feel so great that he sees me this way.

* * *

This semester truly ended with nothing. One thing I have not recovered from: still feeling guilt for aptitude, power, still feeling as though every time things are going well, they threaten to return to bad again. Even when I feel powerful, I anticipate it all falling to shit again. So, of course it does. At the heart, I still don't trust myself, don't think I deserve things that are going well, don't think I deserve to claim what I want. Always think I should want some other thing. Whenever I am so lucky as to find focus, this is the guilt that distracts from it. I feel guilt for a presence I'm worried is seductive, because all discourse seems to verge upon seduction, and all seduction feels violent to me, or at least unclean. But you can stimulate without seducing! And you can comfort without seducing. And you can excite without seducing. You can draw lines of identification without seducing. I don't want to consume or ruin anyone. I am not guilty of anything.

I am going to have to work through discipline in order to bring about for myself a life that, at least, *more closely resembles* that life I'd like to live. I get a reason to live the moment I give myself one.

Slept with Paul again after a dinner party at his house. It was nice: Ivan, Freida, Ruby, more. Ivan made a stew. Didn't love when it became a YouTube party, but, for the most part, nice. Paul had told me of his desire to have a sex night in plain words prior to this party. I wasn't sure; by the party, everything was fine, it met all the conditions I'd wish to set for a casual sex contract. I am never frightened of being myself with Paul. I feel comfortable expressing whatever I'd like, and get satisfactory expression in kind. It's *easy*. Ultimately: I trust him. He is my friend, first, and I trust him. No rules are broken, nothing threatens to be compromised. It is exactly right.

Romance progresses discursively, upon discoveries, upon the power of discovery. In friendship, though, whatever must be known *is* known—certainly there are further depths, but they don't matter; they don't threaten to destabilize the structure. In romance, some party is always a step further, waiting for the other to catch up. In friendship, you stand evenly. In both friendship and romance, *you want to be at that dinner party.*

* * *

It's no pleasure, but it's our privilege, to be disappointed by things. Our disappointment means our rules, too. Depression is a defensive stance when anxiety has become too tiring, and has made us too vulnerable to life.

* * *

Last week, I went to a party of Helena's, which Oreste was in town for. Intimate party: I met their mother. The party was a treat, and it was very easy to speak with Oreste, whom I hadn't been speaking to since his departure. Often we were with each other. He was the last person who spoke to me before I left. Goodbye wouldn't have felt complete without, "Do you want to hang out later?" OK. We did not fuck absolutely instantly like the most recent times. Talking before, and lots more after than usual. What happened was I got everything I wanted. Unbelievably? This certain sort of speech I can't even articulate exactly the nature of had been missing for months, but that evening it wasn't hard to cultivate. Talked about taste and self-cultivation. Talked about how one feels good, and how one feels bored. Talked about what we never talk about (I brought up how I thought it was strange that we never discussed previous romantic involvements). Why should it be OK that I can discuss things with my friends that I can't discuss with the person I'm sleeping with? He says he doesn't even want to hear about his closest friends' old closest friends. We talk about memory and decide that mine is better. He says, at two years old, he was terribly misbehaved. I ask, do you find that you often have feelings while being unaware of them? He says, yes. I tell him, I always know exactly how I'm feeling. He asks, are you kidding!? I say, you know, obviously, I'm kidding a little—but I am almost not even kidding. I bring up all sorts of things, little details I kept, and he is surprised. I tell him, I try to keep a good memory, and sometimes I succeed at this. I tell him I think he idealizes an aesthetic of disaffection, but I don't, and sometimes I feel self-conscious about this. He laughs, really, do you think someone who comes into town for a single night and spends it in your bed only to leave again the next morning might idealize disaffection? I say, it's a possibility! And we laugh, lots. He doesn't like hearing about former attachments because he feels like we're all just substitutes in each others' lives for positions previously held by other people. I say, I don't feel like this.

We're not *together*, and perhaps I've confused, to a point, what I thought I've sought from togetherness. Look, honestly, what scares me is that I care about someone and they do not care about me. That's it. That I'll sleep with someone, and I'll hold myself to a certain standard of treatment with them, and they will not do the same for me. And then they'll meet someone else, a surprise to me, who has whatever thing I happen to lack, and then I'll have nothing left but my loss. This has happened in the past, and I've been heartbroken by it. My suspicion, however, is that a relationship does not inoculate you against these misfortunes. My way of showing care is an anxious one. I want it demonstrated. I want some other scared person to demonstrate skill and fearlessness with me, when maybe this is an absurd thing to want! Because I cannot just—as though I'm not encountering new people to change what I want from the world—pretend as though I have some made-up standard that separates them. The facts: I care more for Oreste than I've cared for anyone in some time. Wrote him later to say it was so nice, and I'm always coming to like him in new ways. He says: "It's a different world in your world (i.e., when with you, at your place), and maybe an important one, certainly a unique one. (These are all good things. OK.)" OK! This is the sweetest fucking thing I have ever been told. "It's a different world in your world."

* * *

Probably: I already know the pleasures and joys I am bound to experience in life. I already know how they feel, what they look like, and, generally, how they are sought. No great mysteries await me. There is no great life I haven't lived but could. I just have to avoid the terrible parts and stay the course of the good, rewarding parts. You have to live in the world you make. It is no great mystery.

* * *

Ivan stayed over on my couch for three nights, and it was splendid. Nice to have company, nice to have someone I feel preternaturally easy around, nice to pepper one's life with that of another for a while. Some dinners, lots of hanging out and chatting while doing other things. A little pot. He showed me that it can be cut with lavender. It's terrific to smoke a light little lavender joint. Blaise sold me, also, a bit of Dexedrine, which I am *smitten* with. This is a drug that makes me feel exactly as I'd desire to. Regular, light, present life with none of that constant-threat-of-the-bed feeling. Suddenly had a good and usable picture of some things that needed to be done. Didn't feel worried or sad, not for a day. What I shall try to do is get my doctor to prescribe me Dexedrine or some similar thing. Considering SSRIs, I worry about the loss of physical passion, the loss of drive. Yesterday, I felt like, should I be able to live like this daily, I wouldn't care whether I had a sex drive or not.

* * *

Why does the most inspired speech seem to always wish to scurry off elsewhere—another register, another genre, another manner, another vocabulary? The artist could always be doing better had she chosen another medium first. The writer would *always* be doing better work had she chosen another style. And meeting a lover, an object of infatuation and inspiration, you'd be better off speaking more like them—or, at least, your desire spurs you forth in this direction. What attracts you is exactly what you aim at reproducing, matching, *beating*. You want your best in you.

Here's my prediction: I have an easier and kinder relationship to some drugs this season. I see no problem with the drugs, which distract me from the suicidal hopelessness that has dominated many labour and leisure hours over the past few months. I hope my therapist has decided that I am only depressive, not bipolar, so she may be comfortable providing me amphetamines. Otherwise, I find it a bit of a joy to smoke some marijuana, and know for certain that I do not deserve even an oil drop of the bullshit of life.

Supposing I care about something right now, it is school, and the friendships incidental to having my attention there. If I do *not* care about anything, it is Oreste. Let us (me) face it: I'm never going to want some other dick as I want that dick as I think of wanting that dick (and I *do*, indeed). Honest about the dick I must wean myself off of, it is necessary to be honest, too, about the steps necessary to undertake. You must go on a blind date with a man about whom you possess no optimism whatsoever, who emails you to say he will be *on time*. OK, sir!

* * *

Dates are shit, life is a bore, pleasure is capricious, and I'm *proud of myself* for smoking the pot necessary to reconcile myself with life!

* * *

For the second day, for the first time, I have taken Wellbutrin. On a prescription. Like one should. I had an appointment with my therapist where I asked, shyly, about being prescribed Dexedrine, "or at least something which would make me feel as Dexedrine felt." When I took Cipralex years ago, I did not like it, and due to fear of Cipralex-like effects, I was not keen on taking any SSRI. I did not want to feel numbed or slowed or knocked out. I just wanted concentration, and to feel stimulated. She told me she would not prescribe a stimulant as a first-line treatment for major depressive disorder, but that on Wellbutrin, some report stimulant-like effects. I'd heard of others using it (Julian, particularly). I decided I could not wait for the good days any longer. So I'm trying it. Began with a very low dosage. It doesn't feel like Cipralex and it doesn't feel like Dexedrine. So far, it doesn't feel like much. But I was tired at a normal hour yesterday, and I didn't have much trouble waking up today, and it's past noon already, and I haven't had the math urge.

Even as I improve myself, I won't get all I want. There is no perfect strategy to life. There is no good way of behaving whereby you can secure yourself against disappointment and pain. It's not as though if I "played my cards right," reserved myself a little more skilfully, I'd attract better the attention I wanted. You suffer then, too. You suffer whenever you want something. Yet you need to want. That's what it is to live instead of spending all day in bed afraid to get your hopes up for whatever or whomever outside in the world may stimulate you.

I often forget how much worse off my body was when I was younger and more afraid. I forget the constant sinus and yeast infections and warts on my feet and nausea and extra weight and every little fucking thing. I forget the hunger, the binge eating, the feeling of bottomlessness. I forget that even though I had a certain resilience, there was always something in the centre of my gut that made me feel so frightened and helpless that it bore out at me from the inside. I never knew what it was. Alexithymia is real. If you speak openly and put your trust in people, it doesn't change your relationship to them, because they don't know the difference. It will all look the same to them. But you will know, and it will feel better physically! Almost as if by magic, to "act naturally" stops one from feeling so sick all the time. The reward, I guess, is not ostensibly positive—in fact, at times it feels painful. It's just the absence of the constantly encroaching physical sickness, something you're easily forgetful of when it isn't with you. This, or my diet's better.

The good is not sought through attachments to lost attachments crystallized in my mind, who actually made me feel compromised even when things were good. The kind of love I want is *so rare*, and it takes such considerable willingness to give on the part of two improbably compatible people who would have to come together upon the most generous luck. The most precipitous. I cannot expect that to be the baseline of life. It's not! It is *the most wonderful fucking thing in fucking life*, and you cannot live it always. All my desire for Oreste is based on nostalgia for three weeks when I thought we would fall in love with each other. They were the fucking best three weeks. I've had special weeks. With Julian, with Max. When two people were giving. When they both truly wanted to be there. When they both made some demand from the other. Then, it stops. You wait for the next time. It will happen whether or not you are "behaving properly," which is one of the generous things about love. It means you don't choose an ethic of behaviour in order to win love, but simply for its own sake. You just establish conviction upon your values in the world, and you just fucking *do* it! It won't always give you what you want, because there is no consistent experience of pleasure. That is not what it is to live. Even in a better life, what is worst will achieve the same magnitude. The state of your silverware might become very important to you. The little things. *You will never live without disappointment, so who fucking cares.*

Possibility is, these drugs are doing a job.

* * *

I have much to resolve privately, functionally. Here are some general prescriptions:

 —Do not play puzzles or computer games to spiral my mind into a pulp of numbers;
 —Do not contact Oreste;
 —Do not use social media websites;
 —Do not masturbate more than once daily (possibly related to Wellbutrin, area feels a bit numb and resistant, anyway);
 —Do not have sex with any man;

—Nothing in your life shall be won having sex with any man. Lots instead lost. Do not have sex with any man, but especially not a creative man, in any field of production. Just enter those fields instead. Imagine I'd never dated any comic. I could be such a very good comic. I make everyone laugh: my therapist, my classmates, my hematologist, and from this I get nothing. People respect performers. This stupid thing of being an artist. Do not address people directly but instead through these disavowedly personal intermediary objects and you are worthy of some sort of stupid respect. Make an enterprise of yourself for being charming and smart, do not just *be charming and smart.* "Working on my art." For whom. Do not have sex with any man working on his art.

There is (slowly) taking the medication to bring oneself to life, and there is working *with* it in order that one not continue to reinforce the habits of a depressed person. I've learned to like jogging. I can learn to like working, doing, socializing again. I want it so every woman loves me and no man thinks to fuck me. I want to be fit and dress nicely, not concealing myself, as I have always known, with long hair, which will grow back since I last cut it. I want to be energetic and energizing, nothing less. And I want to do well in school again, making few mistakes, losing hold of nothing, being ambitious, not allowing things to slip. I want to be my most impressive self. I will allow no attachment who makes me feel excessive or self-conscious for being my most impressive self. I want to be big, sturdy, and reliable. I'll strive for it. It only takes a couple of months at a time and it's not too late. I want to have a true self, a private self, a close self, and some other entity that produces things *for* consumption *with knowledge* of that consumption, separate. Like everyone fucking else. I've already known how to live in an effective way, and I've done it. Do all your readings, write all your papers, and do not have sex with any man.

I am too porous a person, but I won't be.

There has been a cycle in my life: detach myself from others and a feeling of constitution by their interest in me, devote myself to work, do very well in work, feel powerful, self-adoring, large, elated, optimistic—and sadly, in this state, become infatuated. What I must know to do is allow this state to last as long as possible without being punctured by the threat of infatuation, which compresses me back into a smaller, more frightened, more manageable thing. Do not ever again on your fucking life feel good, and big, and centred, and let some insecure piece of shit make you feel self-conscious for displaying "confidence." Do not let it happen again, and do not have sex with any man.

* * *

Physical symptoms of this drug are preventing me from feeling as good as I otherwise might. They are terrible. Writing with a pen: it is hard. Optimism has trouble propelling me anywhere when I cannot bear to be in my own body and I cannot stop touching my face. I'm *most* pessimistic about being the sort of ineffectual loser who cannot live without tweaking. I know this from the clarity it has given me.

Seems so foolish to force stimulation upon a self that is legitimately lacking it. I don't get what I want from the life I've chosen, but there are other lives. Maybe caffeine pills can do until later. Maybe I don't *have* to live a life that leaves me feeling constrained and anxious and stifled.

* * *

Tried to cancel on a dinner with Freida last night but she told me, collect yourself, confirm with me in half an hour; *I want to see you.*

* * *

I have been feeling better, alive, and moved this week. There is a returned pleasure. There is a returned *tone* of pleasure that in depression I forget the feeling of. It is: that things are surprising and mysterious, and that I could happen to come upon some new or fascinating thing at any time. Sensual pleasures are of extreme value to me. I love soft lighting. I love psychedelic and strangely patterned music. I love being on the brink of focus, and I can feel it coming. I really can feel it! I don't know how to get this state back when I *am* unhappy, but you know what? I won't worry.

I don't have a desire to be dulled any longer like I did. I can return to a productive state without feeling as though I'm overbrimming or losing control of myself. I am changing what relationships I put my trust in, and who I'm willing to love. I am losing my desire to be with people to whom I cannot truly explain myself. Or I've lost it. I trust myself in ever a different way and my internal life has changed. Now it is a matter of rebuilding my external life to match it.

Like my body, in better shape than ever, I have to train my mind so that it's mine again. Focus isn't easy. It's a skill; it's trainable; you have to practise it. It gets better; you can lose it. I've been blessed to *have* focus and fascination in life. It's made me lucky to learn what I already have. All I want is to give myself that gift again. *I am an enterprise of what I know.* Don't worry about lost time: there's plenty left. No one can see the years you've lived badly.

Guide and direct: heart rate; attention. It's the only expectation I have from life.

There is a time for feeling pain, hurt, and victimization, but your contract with that victimhood cannot last. How are you to be recognized for your pain? How can someone know it or speak to it? You can choose your friends but living permanently under the sign of distrust will give you little. What if I veered slightly back toward another story I've told myself—that I am hardened, stable, untouchable? It doesn't even matter if it's not true; I can still cling to it. This fiction might do more for me than its opposite. I can still be open and empathetic. I can still profit from all the valuable things vulnerability has taught me without kneeling before the earth as an always-wounded person. To consider oneself resilient is an important step toward actual resilience. It doesn't matter what people have done to you. They hardly know anything about it. You are responsible for the future of what you let into your life.

* * *

There's a reason I'm continually attracted to men who I see as at once constraining and rejecting. Obviously, I guess. It's this qualification held away from you—never unconditional, never welcoming, always with an expectation. I think that by vying after the acceptance of someone I find rigid, I'll find consistency in how I make myself for them. I'll be a *kind of person*. I'll have focus. I'll *be* focused. I'll make myself meet a gaze that, for all its faults, is at least comprehensible.

All summer, and some fall, went to either of two siblings: a screen before the world. Now I'm lost to both, for a period or for always. Who is here to witness me? And who will pay me visits so I don't have to leave my apartment for it to happen?

* * *

The true problem of my life is not a romantic one, it's that my brain is fried to fuck. Depression expresses itself to me as, primarily, a lack of concentration, but I don't have to be depressed to suffer this. I have completely lost the battle with concentration. It takes *so much effort* to stay with something for more than a couple moments before refreshing something on my phone. My fear, my loneliness, my boredom express themselves and find their homes in this flailing inattention. Depression has lifted the injunction to stick to anything off my shoulders. It has released me from the pressure of self-imposed expectation! I've reached, through depression, a momentary calm in mental collapse.

What else: feeling a little *horny* for spring but being unsure who could satisfy it (after asking Paul, who *just* got out of a relationship, and asking Oreste, who is currently in California), I installed Tinder on my telephone to procure prospects for dating or sex. It gave me for some days an optimistic feeling, surprising at the outset, that there was in fact a whole world of available men for me—men of all sorts: attractive, fit, possibly even well-to-do or not so encumbered by negativity. I thought, look at all these! I liked to swipe yes with some of them and chat with a freedom and ease rarely characteristic of my speech with anyone I've already met. The excitement hardly lasted. Went on two dates. Unlike an earlier set-up I had this winter, I had a generous feeling toward both of them. I slept with one, two nights ago, the first time I've slept with anyone since the holidays. But I did not care. He was tall, slim, and handsome, with nice, thick black hair and a very nice dick, but: I did not care. He lauded my sexual *skill* and I think it's strange to put it this way. I felt nothing during. He did not go down on me, which is surprising for someone trying to make a good impression on another in order for the option of more sex to follow (he texted for another session the very next evening!). There is just nothing magical about being penetrated by a person who means nothing to me, who represents nothing to me, even if he is good-looking. And, whatever: charming, lighthearted, seemed kind, smelled of vetiver (I asked). But who cares!

Really, it's just that earlier romantic figures have made me feel so worried about being abandoned that I've wanted to turn away Oreste when he's home, but I love Oreste when he's home, and I don't have anyone else for whom I feel the way I feel for him. Saying no to Oreste will not put a new person I want to be nude with in my life. I want him when he's here. I just have to remember softness, gratefulness, and kindness to us both. Not every action is an investment! I was compartmentalized when younger, but it wasn't all a lie. It was often a utility to me! Sex is not this other thing I do, in another life, which I can get from people I wouldn't otherwise wish to spend time with. It's a special way of relating to privileged people in life whose privilege needn't mean permanence or demand. It's childish that I should forbid from myself something I love because I cannot control how much I'd prefer to have it whenever I wanted. I was better at shutting off those desires when I was younger. Could I have a feeling of separateness back but feel close to myself, too? That would be the sweet spot.

Ah, distractions.

* * *

I feel a perpetual lack of safety, as though there is some *thing* I'll give up by living wrong. I don't have anything to worry about. These have been a stagnant few months. I sacrificed a year of school. I did little. And I considered that "self-care" *should* be what puts you back on the track of your responsibilities and goals, but perhaps if you are feeling sometimes suicidal, one's duty of care to oneself may just be to keep the body living.

I am meant to *work*. But I can't work, I can't think straight enough to work. How am I to write? Constantly, and with a constant failure to produce. Every industry, including those of art, culture, and knowledge production, transforms itself into a market of misery with exhausted, self-hating, labour-obsessed producers fighting over the fantasy of limited space made real by their inability to focus *themselves* upon objects they don't imagine as venerated. This last thing is particular to cultural production. An industry founded upon innumerable hours spent on wasted surplus in search of some *correct* object. Then that very labour is venerated. The misery itself is venerated! The participants in cultural production trust and love the ethic that makes their lives into shit, and they uphold it fervently! Misery sustained on stupid logic of people's supposed capacity for discrimination: if it weren't necessary, I wouldn't submit to it. *Well*.

You don't lose anything by going more slowly or taking a

pause. Protracted adolescence is no problem as long as you don't have kids of your own to raise.

* * *

My course union had our spring social earlier this weekend and, since there was a time cap on the free drinks, I did not get drunk. One classmate, Marianne, was there. She has her mind usually on sex, and her speech usually on sex, and everything has to end there. I left this party to go to one at Freida's, and when I left, Maurice, Morgan, and Marianne were in conversation. Maurice told me later he had some friends waiting at his house but didn't invite her, and I thought, how foolish! But, he said, she hit on me! Everything had to rush to the sex place; little but certain things like she touched his arm a few times too many or she said to him, buy me a drink! I like when men force me to drink!

Marianne complained to me, before I left, women tend not to like me. Young women with other ways to act out do not like her. I *totally* like Marianne, as I tell her and later tell Maurice, because I feel I understand her. I tell him that I suspect hypersexuality is just Marianne's way of working out her power and her powerlessness, and that she's young, and it's likely to be something she feels less of a compulsion toward later in her twenties. He says, it's so prominent for her, the sexual obsession, how could she replace it with anything else? But sex isn't its own discrete category. Sex is just the fantasy of the most intense, direct, and concentrated relation. To want to have sex with everyone is not this special way of wanting everyone—it's just to try to speed up and intensify a relationship in a measurable way. It is to claim the control of another that you are willing to relinquish on your own behalf. It's a contract to be momentarily both generous and greedy, and so often a contract to scatter the moment it is over. Anything that climaxes: you can tell when it's done.

I suspect, as one grows, the need to bring everything to its climax recedes, and along with it the need to give yourself up and have it filled with someone else's self-offering. There are quieter, softer, and less certain ways of being with others.

* * *

Ivan has been in Moscow doing his Russian improvement and Russian socializing. We have a completely unfocused way of communicating with one another. By volume, it fluctuates less based on our level of friendly attachment than by how much we have to share. He'll write long emails because novel things are happening where he is, and I'll write tiny ones with links to things I'm reading. I like my friendship with Ivan, which is non-invasive and free of expectation. It's a weird friendship because of how free I feel to have him around the apartment. He might sublet my room this summer, if I'm away. He's chosen to do his PhD at NYU in the fall (against offers from Northwestern, Princeton, and Stanford).

* * *

I've spent less time, over the past couple of days, thinking of Oreste's return than of Ivan's. We sometimes suggest casually over email that Ivan may live in my apartment whether or not I'm in the city over the summer, and it will be like summer camp. I never think of having sex with Ivan but I like having him around. With Ivan I have someone with whom I can share things in whatever circumstance, who's eager, too, to tell things to me. I don't know why I feel so comfortable having him here when most people make me feel pressured or annoyed. I like how comfortable I am being unadorned before him. I think a sexless live-in partner for the summer would be fun. The right one, Ivan, would be fun.

*　*　*

For the second time in a couple of months, I've felt a lot of pressure on my heart and extreme tightness in my chest, and not during activity or any circumstance where it would make sense to feel anxiety. My grandfather died of an expanding heart? I only learned this recently through my mother's parents, but I don't believe my father would give up an opportunity to tell me his own father died because his heart was too big.

*　*　*

Oreste did come over on his first night back, and it was nice. Relationships, perhaps, may feel just as easy as you allow them to. He was gone, touring. It was comfortable and easy though we hadn't seen each other in three months. I tend toward a certain deliberate (usually sexual) explicitness, which he doesn't love, vis-à-vis written interpersonal communication. But talking is always easy when we're together. We were almost discussing each other as stable figures in each other's lives. By almost, I mean—it was his reference to me, when I told him I felt self-conscious about the ongoing sameness of my apartment, and he said it was nice, a stable base. He isn't someone to exchange letters with, and this is a shame as I do love letters, but he's just *here* (when he's in Toronto). The few months without him allowed me to feel less moved, actually—and not in a bad way! In a way such that I feel not at all anxious. I feel less like a frightened object of his whims and more like a communicative subject with equal whims of my own. There is a point I reach with every object of infatuation where the veil lifts and they stop seeming like the end of men. They feel like one imperfect person whom chance has brought me to, whom I have developed a rapport with.

When does sex cease feeling like the sharpest form of relation? I like the feeling of safety I had two nights ago. I like the idea that we mean a lot to each other, but I know we can't *always* mean a lot to each other, and I always expect that someday I'll just discover he's in a relationship. It's hard to know how to behave with an itinerant who seems both to take comfort in—and also to quite quickly become bored by—any form of stability.

The feeling I love most is of an open, comfortable pliability and sensuality with the world, where days feel good and impressions do, too. And I should never feel prohibited from that. Life doesn't have to be hard or sparing. It can have a bit of intensity all the time.

Intensity—concentration of sensation—as, actually, the only phenomenon of living to combat, in a way, time? It packs in; it can be the emphasis that doesn't *de*-emphasize something else.

The last time I felt good, I just felt, sort of: love. I didn't know for what or for whom, but I felt bloated with it and like it could be granted to anything without being spent—that is to say: exhausted. Language is meant to feel like this, too. You don't lose anything. There is nothing ever to be lost. What I'm describing is more often described as a condition of religious devotion, so I understand the appeal. How does one fill oneself with general, benevolent, non-directed love without claiming it from God? Claim it from whatever. Claim all things good from fucking life.

* * *

Oreste is now the one to have said no. Oreste now considers that our evenings are "too intimate" for a relationship without feeling or commitment, and of course he has neither any feeling nor any interest in commitment. I can't believe he decided this just as I came again to terms with the particular conditions of this intimate contract. I am sad to lose whatever I might have had and sad to have not been the one to make the choice. I feel the loss way. Nauseous, anxious, jittery, confused. Feel like, why the fuck can't I be loved by these men? Feel like, how does one even achieve what they would call intimacy with those they don't want anything from? It's confusing, because I understand that it would feel constricting to be in a relationship with Oreste, so what do I think I want? I just wanted to fuck, longer, the only person who turned me on until he happened not to anymore.

I cried a bit at my desk at the library today. Strange that I would have. Funniest Beckett line, learned today, in prose piece next to "Fail better": "Throw up for good."

There will be those who challenge a positive ethics of plenitude in your life, and you cannot let them shake the faith!

It's unbelievable how anxious I feel at the time of a revocation. It makes me feel *homeless*.

* * *

There were things I forgave by thinking this was the best

thing that intimacy had to offer me right now. Since I'm not in a long-term involvement where sex, trust, and *time saturation* are intermingled, I don't know if it would feel as good as I felt with Oreste all the time. Is a committed romantic partnership necessarily a *new* kind of relation, or is it one where friendly and familial feelings are volleyed with sexual passion? I know nothing is consistent—that no attraction is consistent. I know that in good, companionate romance, periods of revulsion or boredom are still spliced in. It isn't necessarily that you make some new feeling, right? You might just combine and dilute a few feelings you know separately from each other. So, in that case, isn't passionate sexual attraction *the* thing, perhaps the best I can do? (Problem is, men seem quite certain that passionate sexual attraction is the best I can do, too!)

* * *

When I wrote Ivan about the breakup, he advocated that I adopt at least a *touch* of guile. "It took me years to understand you at all." The ways in which Ivan and I are different are important to work through, and important for reminding me of the expectations of the public world, if only to show me just how much of that public world I reject outright and need to separate myself from.

* * *

I still spend each morning I sleep in dreaming about Oreste's cock, but that doesn't mean I'm hopeless or have an unhappy life. It just means I've abstracted some ideal from the time I've spent with him to exactly his size and makeup. But I don't *really* know what his skin feels like, not objectively. I know that I react very well to a certain sensation upon me. Eventually, its form will become fuzzy, and sooner or later the difference will blur and some other skin will feel like just the right skin instead. Like it's always been! It's nice to daydream, even if it seems there's a face to it. It means I'm not actually crushed: I still feel an active, positive sensuality. I still want to be touched.

For two days this week, I felt the enormous, frenetic out-of-placeness that I experienced for much longer at the end of my involvement with Julian. I guess the feeling is heartbrokenness or, rather, grief. A feeling that I am just *about* to lose my footing, like something disastrous could happen now that suddenly I'm not protected from. But to be left with my thoughts isn't actually as bad as the threat seems. Turns out there is little that is actually so bad to think about.

Two nights ago, I had an afternoon tea with Freida that we'd both expected would last an hour or two, but ended up lasting eight. When I told her how terrible I've been feeling lately, she suggested it did not sound like I had a bad mood disorder, but rather a bad life. I cried before her and I was ashamed. Crying before others is unusual for me, but she was calm to witness it. It sounded worse to me that I might not be depressed, but simply *unhappy*. Right—then all I would have to do is make a new life! God willing.

* * *

I did not attend my only final exam but I did get a bursary from having been a better student earlier in my life. Money for a French class at a partner institute overseas. I will go to Paris, hang out with Odile, and then go to Tours for an intensive course. I have trouble speaking French. I become frustrated with my cognitive limits when studying a second language. My memory is never enough for it. I can't tell, when trying to speak French, if my inhibitions are stopping me from speaking as best I can, or if it's just a complete inability to conjure things up. Speaking a second language is a good sort of challenge to face when you're trying to relinquish the need to be found impressive by others, and instead to *learn*.

* * *

I can write a novel full of anxiety, sentimentality, brutality, and sex, and I can even sign it as my own. It's no wonder people are so anxious to make themselves the "artist," because she who articulates always wins. It's Ferrante fantasizing about others' infidelity. It's anyone's comedy. It's whoever makes the art. They tell the story; they command the attention; others trust *them*. Few people are with you and many meander. *You* can be the powerful one who doesn't wait around for others to *recognize how fucking special you are.*

Today a lovely night, first with Caroline, then with Marianne: I adore her. She's younger than me. There is a difference in speaking with younger people. They're unpractised, but on the brink of articulating more. The older one is, the more one forgives oneself for never having articulated certain things; one stops trying. I look at myself: I already feel old. The way I've lost fat in my face over the past couple of years, what I still have in my cheeks droops down. I don't look quite gaunt but I will, soon. I want to share fucking everything.

Maybe there's no categorical difference between some artist and any old person. Or if there is, it's that the artist doesn't speak directly to people; she abstracts her feelings and thoughts into "composed" objects. An artist is someone who's worse, interpersonally, because part of her contract with herself is that she cannot allow her work to suffer by wasting her precious thoughts on *people*. She's far better protected in love if her sentiments reach a confused space between authentically experienced and hypothetical, as if she cannot tell which is which. Always fantasizing about some perfected form of that which she knows, all her life can suffer as though it were lowly and inauthentic. But she's satisfied still because: *that's the world's problem*, and she imagines more.

* * *

Yesterday, had an extended hangout with Max. After my shift at the library, I met him at a bar near the financial core, where he was performing a set. Hanging out was largely on my behest, brought out of recent anxieties over how few of my exes are willing to be friends with me. It's always nice to see him. We've had similarly slow, disappointing winters. I spent hours with him, car-pooled from his set downtown to one at Jane and Finch, and then back to Bloorcourt. Like each time I see Max, it was easy and honest and wonderful. He is a strange figure for an ex, a kind of ideal one, a representation of the fantasy that you really *can* get to know someone you've been attached to openly and intimately once you've given up trying to have a sexual relationship with them. It's odd, actually, how much I feel free to share with Max, or what sort of conversational meanderings pluck out things I wouldn't have expected to say. I like that Max always seems to know exactly what the fuck I'm talking about. Like about pornography and trouble getting off without it (for us both). I mentioned something I'd only told Freida, intimate and a bit mean, that I'm sure I've never been closer to coming with a partner than I was with "not Oreste, but the person before him," during an instance where I was watching him go down on me and he *looked like an idiot.* Max says, "Maybe you're not as submissive as you think!" And then, I: "Uh, *what?!*" Very surprised by this choice of words, confused that he would consider me submissive and believe I considered myself to be so, too. Turns out, terminology borrowed from another man who dubbed me thus, leaving out, I suppose, that I was not *conscious* for the full duration of our fucking. So then, of course, I mention *that*, and we talk about the whole undercurrent of non-consensual sex in Toronto's big barn.

Max and I became quite touchy, staking out space in one of the thousand degrees of being intimate with others, or being attracted to them, albeit only in some minor way that doesn't think of sex at all. I guess, for a few years now, I've felt this way about Max consistently: no desire to fuck him but a lot of affection that is nevertheless physical. It's cuddly. I like being cuddly with Max. I don't know. He's dating someone, actually, still the woman from last fall. I don't want anything *from* Max, or to interrupt or take from anything else in his life, but small and constrained lingering intimacies are such nice things to have. I wish I inhabited a world that didn't consider them so threatening.

* * *

I'm twenty-five today, which is fine.

These passages from Nancy's *Noli Me Tangere* make me sad, but I'm *twenty-five*, and I don't believe in them:

> Far from God, she is without love and allows herself to be paid in order to procure the simulacrum of love. But among creatures there are nothing but these kinds of simulacra. For love is of God; it comes from God; it is God himself in truth.

67

But God leaves his creature to his creaturely abandonment, and Mary is the one who knows to what extent she has been deserted. Abandoned by love, Mary is given over to the simulacrum of love. Yet in that very simulacrum, there is a similarity; there is in the fleeting embrace something which resembles love.

Mary is a sinner; she knows that her caress has no love in it. She knows that her hair is arousing, intoxicating, and without love. She knows that she must not expect anything from either men or herself.

* * *

Have had torrents of social time lately with friends old and new: Freida, Caroline, Maurice, Rebecca, Max, Ruby, etc. Some occasions public, others private, each of a different personal importance. I flip through the diary and see *Oreste*'s name written everywhere and it's just the same thing as *Julian*'s name before. I'm glad sex always matters to me a bit less than before. Everything just takes a name.

* * *

There are limits to pleasure, even the pleasure of smoking pot each day. I feel frazzled. I think I'm the best writer. It is simply that I'm the only person who thinks this. Went out last night to an evening during which Blaise, Marianne, and Paul read. I was feeling some anxiety at this show but mostly I was anxious to have sex with Paul *if* he would, *but* he would not *because* he's trying to conserve himself for the act of writing, until *he's* finished *his* book?! What's worse is I'm next to certain he wasn't kidding about this. Told me that in any case, though, I looked great, like I'd "been working on it"!? It wasn't as though I had some doubt in my mind that he still found me benignly attractive just exactly as he's found me benignly attractive for the last seven and a half years.

Ivan says, other people decide how funny you are, no? I say, no, Ivan, I swear to God I'm the funniest person! I swear on my life that the trouble of it is no one *knows* I'm the funniest one. If only I were the one to do things, then maybe *I* would be the one people would be excited to see. One reason to feel aimlessly excitable is to work too few hours in a week. And smoke pot every day. And to have been recently turned down for sex. When am I least anxious? Because it's not when I'm infatuated with someone who lets me fuck him. It's only during the act of fucking, or the act of being on the elliptical machine, or when reading something that surprises me with a feeling of being at home.

* * *

Here's a joke: at least, safely, I'm doing little in life that I might later be nostalgic for.

No: lots of external life has been missing. I felt clearer, yesterday, neglecting to smoke pot, so today I neglected once again. Irritating emails with Ivan and a shift at the library. Ivan gives me fodder re the life I have to carve an ethic against. All different people add all different things to your life. Let's be honest: two of the things I love to feel are competitive and not quite understood.

The intensely stupid thing Ivan said was that the only way out of a situation in which men are sexually rewarded for their creative pursuits whereas women are sooner punished for theirs was one where the sexual market is upturned totally. That if women no longer hungered for the men who would no longer be asserting themselves more often than those women on the creative-sexual market, women would stop fucking men entirely. He said, if men were not paid in sex for their cultural gifts, they wouldn't produce art any longer. There would be no impetus to do so. Further, since men on the whole would be fucked less, they would become violent. Art, entirely, would change. The cultural items that would be produced on an equalized sexual-cultural plane would serve different functions from before. Many of the features of his bogus consequential dystopia sound to me, in fact, perfectly fine. They don't sound as good to him, recently benefiting from the feeling that his academic career may bring him fame. So he gets greater choice in fucking women he's bound not to care about. Lucky him! If no arrogant dimwit ever wrote again, I'd be glad.

Are there mysteries? Is it a coincidence that this is a man, also, who defends the idea of perfect craft without ever quite articulating what he means? No. No mysteries. You cannot expect men to part with the fantasy of perfected craft when the prospect of that perfection widening their access to sex is the only thing propelling them forward in the cultural sphere.

You are not the only poor, misled person seeking out guidance from the world. For this reason, we must have compassion.

* * *

Last shift at the library until September. I should have been incredibly hungover and somehow managed not to be. A bit of stimulation can sometimes take me very far, and I love to be recognized as smart and attractive.

Depression is a negative ethics: assigning oneself to the threat against oneself, committing to it, giving it the power. Whereas mere hopelessness is something one is bound to feel and, ideally, may float right through.

* * *

Feeling spring in my heels. Blaise programmed a lecturer last night who was exactly my cup of tea, who spoke of *seducing the committee*. He was funny, and had such a way of speaking, and good stories. Started the talk with an anecdote about the tendency to choose a second-best lover out of comfort (so a good seductive tactic is to seduce another by being one's own second-best, so they'll take you without knowing you'd really been their ideal all along). He eventually adapted his understanding through some visual metaphor that no one understood, so I prodded further, and we had a bit of excellent banter during the Q & A, during which he told me that I "simplified seduction to only its most essential elements without a hint of perversion." I responded, "I hope so?" Felt like something I'd always wanted to be told without even *knowing* that I'd wanted to be told it (love). He said seduction is an act of mirroring, and I have always thought of seduction as *active*—drawing another toward oneself rather than drawing oneself into the other. His conception brought with it another element: that the passive subject seduces and joins the dominant object, but in so doing smuggles in some hidden thing, bursting out with it, *becoming* active. After, excited, I went to a bar to read alone, and only thereafter joined the lecture-goers at a more crowded bar at which the lecturer was absent. I don't know exactly what it was, but I felt as though I were glowing, and that anyone near me was bound to be impressed with me, with little effort on my part. I approached the crowded bar and smiled while two men in suits fell to my feet. The smile to them was good, and when they bought me a drink, the rest of me, too, suited them fine. I could play: clever, quirky, sensual, energetic, fun. Just perfectly. I could insult them *kindly* and take pleasure when they talked themselves into a dead end or seemed to feel worried that they sounded stupid. I could say, look at me, talking here to you when there are all these younger, better-looking men around! And it was *fine*, because I emerged forth to them as a Sexy Untamable Woman, and I stuck to the role.

They left. Too drunk. I wanted to fuck someone, so chose someone else named Oswald who had come from the lecture, too. Met him only that evening. Asked, no context, if he'd like to come back to my house. Yes. Took a cab, he paid, we made out quickly, I went down on him but he wouldn't keep erect with a condom on and instead sought to discuss intimate things. That was just not the night I had set out to have. I asked politely as I could, could you leave my apartment? He did. I was drunk, but still wishing for sex, and so fucking sad. That I can't get anyone to fuck me passionately, that my most reliable seductive trait will always be, simply, newness. Can stun some drunk men who don't know I'm more. Less, in other ways. But whoever gets excited gets bored. I felt deeply, primally unlovable this night, and cried—audibly enough that my roommate commented on it. I don't know why I've been so eager lately for just *the act* of fucking. Because I'm leaving the city soon. Because I want to demonstrate to myself that the physical feeling of *Oreste* could be anyone. So far, I've failed. There's always too much time to wait between the lovers that really *do* something to you.

Today, in the park with Freida. Intended to read but instead spoke. She talked about being able to avoid the feeling of intimacy by preserving herself, monitoring her speech, being careful. One strategy: you can't be intimate because you can't show yourself. My strategy: there's no further self I'm obscuring—I have no secret that makes me. All speech I share feels in some way intimate. Equally so. Or equally not. I'm still failing to cultivate intimate relationships while being "true to myself." This makes me feel that the barrier Freida speaks of is similar to procrastinating, or producing intentionally subpar work: if only my *real* talent were on display, then I'd be successful! If you behave in a way you consider natural, if you disappoint yourself in the company of others, you've failed at your best. You don't get the fantasy of self-occlusion—keeping your "true self" hidden so that if only someone would have known it, they'd have loved you more.

* * *

I've had: days. Empty time, sexual misadventures, drinking, hangovers. Not a surplus of reading or thoughtfulness, but that can wait, certainly. I can't imagine the number of things that are inspiring my feeling of sexual desperation at present, but there are plenty. Ran into older friends from adolescence, drank. It's been a decade now since I first met these people, and in some ways I feel like I have no better status in the world than I did then, at fifteen. I work on fewer creative projects and people aren't as quick to be with me. Then: a number of generous, unsurveilled friendships with people whose nerves were more active around others than with me, because I had little to judge and little to return. Occasional wit and a captive smile were my gifts.

I've come to know that having my own speech engaged by someone else's in an equitable way is more stimulating than being on the receiving end of a monologue. I'm still, probably, quicker to laugh than the average person, but I'm positively *stolid* in comparison to myself as a teen. Sex isn't the same as then, of course. I feel as though simply my capacity to reject others makes me rejectable. Say that very same Julian I met, then, when he was twenty-seven, were to meet me *now*, at twenty-five? Would he have fucked the person I am today as the person I was then, or would he be considerably more nervous doing so?

Another day there was also a Max thing with kissing. Many small things and no good, hard fucking, like when I was a teen who could be shown to want exactly what was given to me.

* * *

I suppose I'm far from the only woman who uses television in order not to be alone with her thoughts.

* * *

Last Friday night, I spent a few hours with Helena, and this was a pleasure. We spoke mostly about the nature of pleasure, happiness, and desire. We move through these subjects *very slowly*. I have some recurring fantasy that when Helena and I got together to talk, we'll discuss Oreste, and I'd get some perspective or closure from this, but we didn't discuss Oreste, for whom Helena is not, in fact, here to provide me perspective on. It might nevertheless have been easy for her to detect something of a summary when I explained how sexual compatibility was rare to me, and that I was so inexperienced in any other way of being with another romantically that it was the only thing that mattered to me. She said that, for her, there's a whole other, transcendent *way* she hardly even knew before her current partner.

One thing, a bit suspicious, was that when I'd mentioned how much I enjoyed last summer, and she said, "Really? I got the idea that you were not having an easy time." This caught me off guard. She knew!?

* * *

I still feel like a depressive—or at least someone with significant fatigue issues, but for a few days I've been better. I'm not drinking heavily or smoking pot (I had been drinking *so heavily*); no math puzzle craving; no sleeping around; no trying to call or text Oreste late at night, which I earlier did multiple times to no benefit whatsoever. These are things I already know give me nothing but nevertheless give off the *scent* that something fortuitous might come from behaving badly, as it often felt when I was younger. If, between fifteen and twenty, everything happened by magic when I was drunk, shouldn't I try to reclaim that magic? No. Because I'm better, clearer, and saner when sober now than I was during those years, and all it looks like is either the vacillation of some nutcase or that I really *am* that idiot at heart, which is not what I want anyone to think of me, in truth: that I'm foolish, that I'm scared, that I'm insecure, that I'm small. It's true that some men would love an opportunity to exploit loyalty from those qualities, but fuck if those are the men I've learned to court!

I thought, during adolescence, that my private life would anchor me to the world, and that attracting others to me would make me safer. It's not true. It just provides me disappointment and pain. I only know the pleasure of the interpersonal better than the pleasure of work because I've spent more time with it. However. I'll find the same intensity of pleasure in work. I'll develop the same masochistic attachment to one success for nine rejections that others have been able to—

staying hungry, working, devoted, aching. Because *that* adds up to something. Some person, in the end, will add up to shit.

* * *

Setting up plans for the rest of the summer. Feels great. Know exactly when Odile's home and that I can stay with her in Paris and that we're both so excited. Going to spend some time at the residency with Ruby, too.

* * *

Met Caroline last night, had average-tasting dinner, quick walk in pouring rain to her friend's house. We watched some sci-fi series she's been into on Netflix while I flipped through a copy of Ayn Rand on selfishness, which I found on a shelf. Nathaniel Branden, identified as a contributor but not as Rand's protege or lover, had a few short essays. Read his piece on the psychology of pleasure while thinking about Fourier, thinking about what corruptions of pleasure wouldn't be deemed so in societal harmony. So too in Branden's concep-tion, virtuous pleasure is formally distinguished from vice— *pleasure doesn't seduce us.* It is, indeed, every human's driving force. It's just that whatever the pleasure is that happens to attract someone reveals the soul of said person, their lived set of values. Whoever loves lowly, destructive pleasures will lead them to disaster, and whoever instead enjoys produc-tive labour and high art will find through his pleasure a very good life. It's a funny coincidence how little either Branden or Fourier, totally opposite each other on the socio-political spectrum, should speak of discipline or its need. In either conception of humanity, a good, free person doesn't need it. Unencumbered in either case from a certain set of contem-porary demands (capitalism, socialism), the subject is bound to be his best self, and he can follow his pleasure someplace good.

Still, for Branden, there are pleasures that don't qualify— false ones too easily indulged in. There's something that *feels* like pleasure, but then there's something else that *is* pleasure, and they both have the same name.

What if I want to change the kind of life I live and relationships with friends and lovers where we are both, above all, silent? I wouldn't want a silence that means stoicism, because there's nothing ethical about that. I want a silence that means comfort, that one's needs are being met, that one isn't hungering for anything.

One utopian model: seeking a life that best facilitates stimulation/mania—but isn't this, too, a little anxious? What about the utopian desire to be happy in silence—a silence that doesn't feel stifled but *satisfied*. So *unhinged* is a utopia that wishes to always feel hunger.

If I only seek out true pleasure and never read garbage on the internet again, I can make prattle my past life.

What if there's nothing complicated about an ideal life: it's just a comfortable bed, a big, clean kitchen, and the humility to really give *Mind Over Mood* your best shot?

In other news, I could swear that one teen boy in a car of several just said to me, "Fuck our jizz," but that couldn't have been it.

* * *

As per style this spring, got too, too wasted drinking with Marianne and hastily tried to sleep with a friend of hers. I think I was being bossy all night, impatient with any men who wouldn't defer to me flaunting the sheer power of sexiness, because I was wearing something revealing in a flattering colour. I didn't quite black out, but still, eventually, we could have been talking about anything.

I have a desperate sexuality right now relating to anxieties over my expiration. I see myself as lacking the particular vulnerability I never understood made me attractive when I was younger. I wonder: is there some quality I don't even know of, which I possess *now* and won't be able to get back later, too? I couldn't possibly be so idealistic forever, nor so lost. That isn't even to mention the pertness and tautness I'm losing daily. My breasts will only continue to deflate; my thighs and stomach will only continue to wrinkle; my hair will keep getting coarser, and it will keep going white. What I don't use will go to waste, and I have to profit somehow off myself before it's too late. I feel the injunction to use myself for "profit" in a way mixing the French and the English usages. I want to use my body and being for the best experience of pleasure before it changes and I'm bound to experience different kinds—and I want to use it over others in order to get things from them: admiration or drinks or the occasional place to stay.

Still, I know there's not much that is more attractive than softness. I just don't know how to play soft anymore.

Part of growing older and seeing youth go is an infantile insistence on keeping it, wishing for the passions that can be invigorated by juvenile behaviour. But it's not flattering, plus it brings more pain to life. When I was drunk again, I *still* called Oreste, because I thought that if I didn't take the opportunity to accost him while drunk, I wouldn't do it sober. Oreste has not indulged me in the idea that he might like to see me since saying he didn't want to sleep together anymore two months ago. And though my ideal is a considerably more generous approach, this is immaterial.

I'm not entitled to the generosity of anyone. A childhood with negligent parents can lead to an adulthood anxiously trying to prove the beholdenness of others you've come to know, but the truth is there's no one with the responsibility to you that your parents once had, and even if you didn't get it then, you're *still* not owed it later. That is simply the bad luck of living. I'm not entitled to the attention of anyone, even if they'd earlier chosen to give it. They are liable—and they have every right—to retreat, ignore, cut off contact, anything. Whether it's due to boredom or carelessness or self-preservation or anything doesn't matter a touch. It's not up to them to explain things to me if they don't desire to. I suspect that, as much as dating older men so young did its number on me, it gave me a false precedent: being cared for by men too guilty to abandon me totally, lest I feel used. It's cooed me into a false standard of closure that doesn't represent how many people come apart from each other once they're both adults. People simply say goodbye and cease to seek any comfort from the other, and have some fucking discipline and put their libido somewhere else, or suspend it indefinitely, if that has to be done instead. No one owes me a thing. I simply owe it to myself to move on gracefully from those who've denied me.

If it happens that two of the more important things in life are respect and patience, then life is indeed somewhat less fun than otherwise. But how fun has it really been so far? Has my long, lonely, indulgent, and insecure young adulthood really been so much *fun* for me? What, really, do I have the pleasure of feeling? Cute, quirky, attractive with strangers, and though loved by those closest to me, loved always with the understanding that there's *something in me* that will never be settled, will always seek to move, often toward rejecting people—something destined for perpetual unhappiness. I think I'm so fucking good and generous, when such a good deal of what I consider pleasurable consists of seducing others against their better judgment! For a decade now, I've wanted people to be captive to me not because I wanted a future with them, but because I simply got off on my hold upon them. It's supposed to be some fucking coincidence that whatever the situation has been—queasy involvements, affairs—I've probably spent barely a month having anyone with me not because of a frisson of lust, but because they thought they *should* be? Such a fucking generous woman—if I'm not turning people against themselves, I'm not turned on for a minute! The core of my sexual identity is fucking rotten. It would be no surprise to me if the rottenness made it so that I didn't understand how it worked for others at all. Should it be any wonder that I am orgasmically impotent with others despite performing with no trouble when I'm alone? It's not. It's from a dishonesty with myself and others. To sit there fucking like I'm so good and free when in reality so much of what I want is to be the woman with the tits to destabilize a man because: a) I've never gotten what I wanted; and b) I'm not about to be getting it there. What I've delusionally convinced myself is that openness is rather impatience, and a disrespect for the boundaries others have drawn for themselves. I'm an embarrassing person who's never come to terms with it who's had the good fortune of some months that were good.

It's valuable to you if no lover is to treat you like a child again, and it's about fucking time. Do not embarrass yourself. Do not beg for crumbs of attention if you think you can pressure others into giving them to you. If you take others seriously—their lives, their decisions—perhaps it will come naturally that you begin to take your own life seriously, too.

I fear being empty, because nothing seems worse to me, but that's not quite the issue. I'm not empty, but disorderly. I have got a shit ton of interiority, but as it's still in disarray, it pulls all this garbage in, and it's always begging. *People know and recognize the pressure of those in disarray.*

I think I'm recognizing how megalomaniacal even a quiet person can be. What is my depression? It's: impotence in the face of the non-correlation of the outside world to what I want. Every once in a while, the depression seems to lift because for a time I feel my sensibility is being recognized or repaid or I'm getting fucked well and often (which is a form, perhaps, of the same thing, or at least can feel as though it were so), but the truth is, these are flukes, and I do not and will not live in a world dreamed up exactly according to my standards. What is my depression? It's the narcissistic precedence given to my own desires and their uncedability to a world that doesn't match them. It's an obsession with control, and a complete collapse before the imperfect reality of living. Seen this way, my depression could easily be overcome were I only to give some of this up.

* * *

I feel, in fact, a little: sick, rejected, worried, aggravated, unsound. But do you know what? I suppose this is better than the number of days I went this year feeling next to nothing. Smothered, sleeping, ignoring myself, passionless without even the desire *for* passion. I was contained but I was fuck-ing *asleep*. If now, perhaps, the drunkenness and the misbe-haviour and the wandering about and the conscious nervous sadness makes me feel that I'm having an episode of a kind? I daresay I prefer it. I needed *something*.

If the fucking worst I did was text Oreste late in the night and also try to sleep with someone else in person, good fucking grief. Oreste said I was harassing him. He had never said this before. *OK*. I won't do it again.

I think, if you can handle it sober, it's useful to endure the kind of anxiety I've been feeling lately. It springs me into fits of thought that never quite feel proper, or logical—they feel too sentimental, they feel obsessive, they feel simply *overpowered*. But if the choice is between that and what feels like a void of consciousness? OK, let's be serious—these are not the only two choices. But they are, indeed, *two of the choices*.

* * *

While I was working at a café, some man approached me so that he could show me the journal entry he'd drafted about me the afternoon before. Curious, of course, I told him, please! It went like this: a young woman, wearing sneakers, has walked in reading a book I can't make out the cover of. But, it said, I've just recently met this *other* woman, whom I feel good near, and who is attractive but perhaps not *beautiful*, and has character, yes, but perhaps a little too much, and I don't know if she is the woman I envision at my side in life. And then, the antidote? Me, who hadn't spoken! Who was softer; *magnetic*, not seductive; and *truly beautiful*, not simply cute (and, indecipherable as I was, with no obnoxious surfeit of *character*). Disgusting. This idiot rejecting man with his fantasies who did not know that I was the too-much woman, and that to spend only an evening with me would send him back again, looking for another chesty young thing, with a book, whose voice he hadn't heard.

* * *

I feel, again, as some lucky times previous: like I give a shit about no one. Just no particular invested shit. Before I was horny, reckless, and binge-drinking like crazy. Now I hardly give a shit about surprising myself with some hidden experience of wonder at all!

 I spent a long, lazy night at Max's on Saturday. If I'd have been asked years ago, such a night with him would have been ideal to me: lazing around, chatting, watching TV, reading or working together, and eventually sex mostly by his urgings. It makes almost no impression on me now. I like Max, and we respect each other, but I feel ultimately when I'm with him like I have so much more to say than he can begin to understand. We're *comfortable* together, but we pose no challenge to each other. He's too distractable to pay any attention to most of what I have to say, just as he's too distractable for *anything*, and it's no fault of mine! What I liked about spending so many hours with him (around 5:00 p.m. one day to 3:00 p.m. the next) was that I was less attentive to my telephone and ashamed to be as distracted as I would have been were I alone, but *his* distractability is too stubborn to settle down, even in my company.

I don't regret the fucking, but the fucking with Max is never the fucking I want most, and I've known this for some time. Like me, he's accustomed to porn, and he's so used to masturbating that he cannot come without jerking himself off for a *while*. My fucking someone does not hinge upon sitting there jerking myself off for a while! He is not taking me for a good ride there jerking himself off. That's not the experience I want to have fucking. It's just not the sex I want. I'm too *conscious* for it—my mind is in completely the same place; the experience is totally non-transformative. It doesn't *do* anything. That's not the point of fucking. That's just no way I want to be fucked.

All the same, merely *being around* him reminded me of Julian, and reminded me of all the hours I spent grateful to be witness to his life rather than to be out having my own, or to be working, or to be attending to my problems. When I ask Max questions, he hardly ever returns them. When I was with Julian, I never wanted him to. I don't desire this way of being with another anymore. I don't get anything but a fleeting feeling of comfort from it.

There is nothing to be sought from sex. Stop watching porn so that when I *next* meet someone who stimulates me, who I really want to fuck, I can train myself to get off with *him*, and on being with him. And then what? So I come with him? Is this going to be the cure to my relational life? Fuck no, and many skipped orgasms in the meantime. So onward instead, jerking off to this absurd image of the ecstatic that I've become so comfortable with. I hope I never want to fuck anyone again. When I don't, and when I'm without all the attendant anxiety and longing and confusion that comes with it, life really is better. Or life is at least without so much of the nonsense.

One *should* experience stress in life—at school, at work. When I have a system of disappointment and happiness that rewards hard work and clarity at school, *that is good.* No disappointment in love is going to teach me anything but to desire with greater caution.

The whole fuck-world causes me undue resentment, rage, and pain—and it's all avoidable by putting my efforts and attention back to academics, where they belong. Fucking will not give me a life. Learn from the wisdom of the fucked-over women who've learned to lead better lives and, if you must go on any date, take advantage of an opportunity to be out in public socializing with a man who wants to impress you because gender binaries often still seem real and he really does think sex isn't something you're going to want to offer him unless he wins it somehow.

Even my most generous thoughts about Oreste were about the cleanness of my relationship to him as this total abstract: that in him, first, I sought something that wasn't prohibited from me (outright), that I wasn't afraid to talk to him (for as long as this was so), that I didn't seek social mobility through him (only, subconsciously, through his sister). Who *he* is is conspicuously absent from all of this, and for all my musings about how I'd finally made improvements to my desire, I barely wanted to consider: 1) for whom; and 2) the absolute separateness of his own desire from mine. This might just be what infatuation *is*: an attraction that invents its own object while blind to its true qualities, and a denial that the object has some hidden desire that you can neither perceive nor accommodate. Infatuation can make you feel high and it can make you feel good, so you stick to it, but it's a kind of psychosis, so you give it up.

The thing is, I know that under the bullshit that muffles it, the dick in my head is not the problem I must solve. The problem of my life is that I'm purposeless, often, and when I do have purpose, I can't control my wandering mind, and I feel a loneliness I think social media can cure; I'm so scattered. Sometimes I have bad discipline and I don't exercise, and other times when I have good discipline and I *do* exercise, I hastily confuse the sensual pleasure I feel with *sexual* pleasure.

Scientists publish that your neuro-emotional development is not complete until twenty-five, and I'm going to behave as though this fact is essential.

How about, as a potential narrative for my life: there was the origin (childhood) and then the wound (adolescence) and then, briefly, the recovery and first try at adulthood. Then there was, for years, as is traditional, *the analysis*—lived publicly, through literature, discourse, and reenactments. And then the true adulthood, now the pact with myself to put things back together, as it was necessary that they unravel in order to bring the wound to light. Ego is nothing if not complying with the injunction to behave in one's own interest without setting traps for oneself. And the *good* superego is as a parent understanding and kind, who only wants what's best, and doesn't want to punish. I've been swimming in id for years now. It's not necessary to continue.

Utopia

I AM ON A PLANE AND I AM FEELING RATHER GOOD. CALM and optimistic. I took transit to the airport, waited for no one, and experienced no anxiety on anyone else's behalf. I was exactly on time, moving at just the pace I like. I feel good and light. I have curiosity and optimism without any feeling that I'm brimming over. At noon tomorrow, Odile will meet me at the Gare du Nord. I may not sleep before this. In the evening I'll have dinner with Claude and stay over at his apartment, and the next night Odile is playing a show, and I'll stay at her place. If her boyfriend is uncomfortable with me staying over too many nights, I will be tossed around between apartments, but in all cases there will be someplace for me to sleep. I have no worry at all. Air travel's incredible. The wine may be free. God is fucking real.

Max stopped by the house this afternoon while I was packing to get the key to sublet in July. I had inadvertently seen him two nights earlier, when I was at the Three Speed with Caroline, and he was ostensibly on a date with the girl he told me he'd broken up with a month and a half prior. Having so recently slept with him, I felt misled witnessing this date, and in being introduced to Cybil, I mostly felt embarrassed, and also a bit stoned, for I had just at that moment biked in from a joint with Maurice/Rebecca/Dylan over euchre. I may have been curt, and I don't know the extent to which Cybil knows my *friendliness* with Max. Apparently that night had been their second date since a possible reconciliation, the first having been the previous Wednesday, three nights before we fucked. While I feel it was an ethical misstep to initiate sex with me knowing he was becoming involved again with his former steady, I didn't feel jealousy, or anything. What I mostly feel is patience, and a knowledge that Max is between things, seeking attention, lonely and flailing.

Who else is having a life. My mother. I had lunch with her today, which I had to chase her down for. She has not been feeling well. Trouble at work, trouble in life, trouble with the family we share. She says she has, in fact, been inconsolably depressed for weeks, and her doctor upped her Wellbutrin prescription, but she doesn't know what happened, for there seemed to be no trigger for any of this. I felt my heart sink through the week when she was putting off dinner plans by the day, and worried that she'd already stopped working. She hadn't: she's there, but how long for? I want my mother not to give up on a life that has some structure and order, because I know the alternative will be worse.

Last night, Blaise organized a reading with Marianne, Morgan, and me. He proposed this when I hit him up for two weeks' worth of pot and told him I'd been working on things and wanted a place to read them. He just says, I'll start a speaking series! There he did. The others he chose, close to him, too, were fantastic. Each of us had something so much our own. I wrote a meditation on attachment to an empty sign and a stuck life and what loyalty means when it's less to a person in their particularity than to some invented form in one's head that has to do with nothing more than an abstract eagerness for touch, together with a distrust that a touch under any other name could be right. I want to make others feel like I've explained something they lack the words to describe. I want to open up ways to think about desire. There wasn't a single man I cared to seduce in the room, and I felt fucking great. There was a man who I know edits a literary magazine I sent the story to earlier this week. In another life, I'd want him to want to fuck me. Now I want him to publish my fucking story! Dylan came, and later we biked up to see Maurice and Rebecca, who had earlier been at a wedding-rehearsal dinner. We each had a rose gin and tonic (the fucking most divine thing), shared a joint, and played cards. No one got drunk, I didn't come home sad that I wasn't fucking anyone, and these are my fucking friends for life. It was my last night in Toronto for two and a half months, and I couldn't have asked for a better one.

* * *

Arrived. Spent the night at Claude's because Odile's relationship with Anton has become bumpy, and she expressed queasiness at having me at her apartment two days before I left Toronto. I expected that if I asked to stay at Claude's apartment, he would try to sleep with me, and I was correct. Earlier, surprisingly, I had a very lovely time with him. I was received at the train station at noon by Odile, who took me to lunch before bringing me along to her friend's house. I was completely exhausted, certain we would not be stopping by her and Anton's. I asked Claude if I could stop by his place a couple of hours earlier than planned, to nap, and he said yes, and there was simply no substitute for this—I don't know what I would have done without it. For a couple of hours, he worked and I slept, neither of us disturbed, until he woke me to walk down to the Bastille for Moroccan food. Bizarre that he chose a restaurant an hour's walk from his apartment by Crimée, but the walk was lovely, full of my memories of the Parisian northeast, and he was lovely to talk to. In the past he'd been exhaustingly didactic with his Marx and his Hegel, and considering the demands of the graduate program he moved here for, I expected even worse, but got instead, thankfully, conversation.

We spoke personally—of goals, relationships, family—in articulate terms. Claude is physically beautiful, mostly in just the ways I like: small, compact but strong frame, a nice mouth, slightly too much hair on his head. He's smart, and sometimes very stimulating for me, but there's just *something*. There's a certain warmth toward him I lack totally. I really do not feel attracted to this person who by all accounts it would make sense that I would be attracted to. I could give this lack of attraction *reasons*—sometimes I think he is a bit emotionally stupid, unaware, patronizing, not always respectful—but these qualities have not stopped me from being attracted to others! Maybe it's that they coalesce in Claude to a degree of masculinity that is unbearable. Maybe it's that in all his free avowal of affection for and attraction to me, I don't see any vulnerability in him. I just think of him as a playboy.

But: conversation was great! Nice discussion of Catholic versus Protestant ethics. It brought clarity to certain ideas I've had about the religiosity that seeks God in others—in ritual and presence—rather than a private, elected relationship to a supreme impersonal essence that doesn't have much to do with life on the ground, more concerned with cleanliness and abstinence. I'd earlier thought this latter sort might be the default for irritating, intellectual, late-conversion Christians, but it might be just Protestantism rather than Catholicism. It was great! And when he kissed me by the canal, I was happy for it; I smiled and enjoyed it. He kisses in a way that's compatible with me, and he held me with a force I liked a lot. It was, in terms of pure sensuality, better than any embrace I've had in some time, but it was just, I don't know, *without*.

I had no idea how to return to his apartment and not fuck him since I'd been active in kissing, and how I did this was: passively and gracelessly. I just stopped responding to anything, but this did not make *him* stop, because I suppose nothing makes certain people stop, short of saying, *stop*. He didn't force fucking, and he didn't take out his dick, but he did, sort of, just continue kissing and humping for so much longer than I would have expected one could without garnering a response. What became most alienating to me was that he could continue to be turned on despite my inactivity and my occasional slaps of his hand from my panties. I collected myself and told him that it wasn't working for me, that this is not how I behave when I'm "feeling the way I usually feel doing this," that I'm normally aggressive! He still went at it, again. Some moans of my name. I resented that he did not stop when I made it verbally clear I wasn't comfortable, and I wasn't about to fucking *reward* him for this.

Maybe I'm not attracted to Claude because he is the sort of person who can go on like this. I preferred the physical sensations of being with Claude to those of recently being with Max, but Max brings out such lightness and affection in me. For all the hours of talking we did last night, Claude didn't bring out any. I slept better next to Claude than I would have next to someone I cared for, and we woke up late this morning. I packed up my things, Odile finally in her apartment to welcome me. When at last I arrived there, it was lovely! She and Anton made a nice, late lunch. The apartment is beautiful, bright, back in Montreuil. Since then I've walked into the city along routes I remember, not terribly affected by last night's discomfort. It's sunny. Pyramids of baklava and basbousa flood out of the convenience stores onto the street. I like being flooded with memories even of uncertain, lonely times. It makes me feel familiar, and like I have some sort of home here, even when, in truth, I don't. I am now dependent on those I know the city through, and they are kind to let me stay with them. I can sit in a room alone all I want once I'm in Tours for my next course.

I know my desire is not making *choices* (it certainly isn't making many good ones!) but I think there is some intuitive judgment about the vulnerability of the other at the heart of it. In Claude, who is smart, beautiful, and quite sexy, there's just this sort of improvised affectedness that's missing. I just feel like he's never surprising himself, always saying something prepared, unreliant upon me, that he was ready to say prior. And though I do become attracted to people who vacillate and reject, I don't ever become attracted to those I see as truly untouched by me. I like the stumbling, the inadvertent jokes, the speech obviously conjured anew, the guileless (if noncommittal) "It's another world in your world."

Despite my romances going, by and large, badly, there *is* something a little vigilant about my desire. Before any kiss, I mentioned to Claude (unexpectedly!) that there were certain people for whom I'd always have a feeling of lingering erotic warmth (and so, too, would always value the same feeling in kind). It's a changeless feeling of privileged warmth that no interceding love or infatuation can take away, that can always be invigorated. It's a way of colouring these people that supersedes any feeling of debt or betrayal or resentment. What forms it is unclear—but I think it involves a mutual puncturing. There's a certain kind of warmth I'm never going to stop feeling for those I've been nude with who've displayed vulnerability with me, and who came to conclusions in my presence they wouldn't have come to if I weren't there. I want the vulnerability of someone who goes *soft* if he thinks he's being denied, not the self-invigorated lover who then gets harder and doubles down.

Oh, very funny line way back one week ago from night walk with Max in the park, talking about jerking off. I said that in my case there's no filth, no product, and no feeling of exhaustion for having made any. Max said to this: I wish every time you came, a little bit of my come came out. This was a very funny and wholly surprising thing to hear him say. Romantic in a very strange way. The funniest exchange of my evening with Claude was when, excited for discourse on the street, I asked, "Oh my god, when we get back to your apartment, do you want to sit and read for, like, three hours?!" and he said, "No?!"

* * *

Life is fast. Tonight I move to Villejuif for a short while to make some room for Odile's romantic strife. Last night at a party after her show, I met a lovely young American named Miles. He is going to Tarnac on Monday. I am going to some Marxist *banquet* in Levallois-Perret he invited me to, today. Last night I gave him a blow job in the bedroom of the house where the party was. This was fun to do. Last night, also, one of the young women at my reading wrote me to say she can't get my story out of her head. Life is so large out of one's bedroom. This afternoon, after Odile left the apartment, has been the first time I've actually been alone since arriving (I have been by myself in cafés and on the street, but of course there is another way in which this couldn't be further from *alone*).

* * *

If there's any more appropriate way to spend Father's Day than in a flophouse with a bunch of itinerant communist (criminals?) in Île-St-Denis, I'd have to be made aware of it. I am currently feeling appropriately open to one sort of terrific life, a communistic one with little need of privacy. Who did I have sex with? Was it Miles? Yes. Once yesterday early in the evening and once this morning prior to the group's departure to Tarnac. Yesterday, after spending the morning with Odile, I packed up enough for a few nights elsewhere and took the metro from one terminus to another to Levallois-Perret—a suburb I'd only ever visited to babysit for a very well-to-do French family—for a sit-in in front of an intelligence agency. Lazing people, food prepared, eighteen-to-thirty-five demographic. I arrived near the end, and Miles, who had written me an email to invite me after we met the night prior, had just woken up from a nap on the grass. I met a few friends and was reminded of the names of a couple of others from last night—Hector, Roman, a lovely PhD dropout from Montreal named Sophia, and her partner, Phillipe. Two Swedish girls. Two American girls? Miles, Hector, and Roman are all American, from the South. They're clever, driven, political, *mysterious*. Of the three, Hector is the youngest, perhaps only twenty-two. Roman is, by the look of it, twenty-five to twenty-seven, the funniest one, moved from Atlanta to Sweden, the wiliest of them, the criminal, the liar. Miles is twenty-six, does building projects in New Orleans, will do the same here, the most polite, did the most cleaning at the homestead, handsome, big eyes, very muscular chest and arms, light hair. Everyone is clean, well-dressed, and shaven although they live in a certain sort of squalor, to which we took a very convenient bus.

So often, I idealize being with others, but when actually *finding* myself with them, I don't want to stay for long—the demands of the interpersonal become something to retreat from. But this group had accustomed themselves to being with one another in a way that wouldn't demand retreat, and I found myself at home. After our arrival to the house, any one of us could do just as we pleased: chat, pass books around, cook, play cards. Miles and I excused ourselves to an only slightly more secluded room for a fucking, and, honest on my life, one of the Swedish girls had—just as he was about to come—played "Heart of Glass" on the stereo. There was no, what am I doing here? Simply by being there, one could do anything. I met only one person who actually lived in this house, Patrick, from the pacific northwest, who studies philosophy at L'Ecole normale supérieure. He keeps the doors unlocked, and friends from the neighbourhood filter in and out all day, including this fun little kid, Moussa, couldn't be older than nine, who would come in and joke with us, scribble adornments on protest signs with markers, try to persuade us to play soccer with him. The communists' relationship with the children of the neighbourhood was primarily established, I'm told, by buying fireworks from them. Hours passed between undemanding activities, and I never got bored or antsy. Final conversation of the night with Sophia, Miles, Hector, Patrick, on Fourier and Lacan and desire and attachment and action. Everyone came at praxis from some different place. This morning while fucking, Miles joked with me, as he struggled to put curtains up, that he was *not* a Fourierist. I said, no, me neither! Nothing bothered me. In this environment, I was hardly ever hungry, hardly felt I had any needs to meet—I ate a little tabbouleh and had a tiny beer, a little wine, all

night—no coffee in the morning until after I left, no cigarettes. Above all else, I just had no feeling of *demand*.

* * *

It is later, and I have fucked two such different Marxists today. It could be said that I am living one among the dreams,
but it is a very strange dream. They both talked to me with
deference about Fourier, who has become my party trick.
What an obvious choice for a cute, quirky, eccentric party
trick for sex. The second Marxist was just Claude. If you look
at someone sucking your tits for long enough, it is likely to
become pornographic. Life is stupid but not absolutely bad.
Not distinctly. What I would like is *two* fans. If I think of a
joke while cuddling, but, out of politeness, remain cuddling
instead of going to jot it down and then lose the joke, I feel
cheated.

* * *

I feel such a quick and resigned flexibility to my present circumstances. This trip is not what I expected. Odile, since last
time, is *different*, or at least in a much more tumultuous time
in her life. So I cart my things around Paris, or rather around
its environs, thankful that I nevertheless *do* have places to
stay, and if some of those places have been contingent upon
sexual exchange, at least it's been with people I've not been
totally repulsed by. This afternoon, again in Montreuil, I slept
in after Anton went to work and Odile went to visit her therapist, before going down with a packed suitcase to Villejuif
to a house of her band friends where she'll also be staying
for a short break from Anton—which will be the beginning,
presumably, of a lifelong break from Anton. In the midst of
her breakup, she has been kind enough to ensure that I have

someplace to sleep, but also, I think, has not asked me a single question about my last two years in Toronto. I'm a single woman floating around. She has a passionate distractability.

I haven't yet spent any time anxious to be alone, which is strange to me—it's as though something from my natural disposition has gone missing. I am feeling open to almost anything, spending time with others who seem in a similarly open mood. Arrived in Villejuif today: new, foreign, faraway neighbourhood. Odile's friends, who were to let me in, were not yet home. There was a dog on the property, which I hadn't been told, but she had a very playful disposition. Somehow my emotional state took no detour for frustration or anxiety—*When will they be home? What am I doing? How long will I be here? So much I haven't planned!* I just *played with the dog* like a sensible person, and then, when I was distracted by the animal, they arrived. I dropped off my suitcase, which I had carried across town for the third time, and we left the house again at once. They loaded their things into a van and asked if I wanted a ride to the metro. I said, no, it's right there! And Alexandre said, yes, but this will be funny. And I said, OK, OK, I want to do the more fun thing.

There is a fantasy to my attraction to Miles. He is a leftist who *lives by the theory.* Living takes precedence over the theory. He builds, and he's strong. He's interesting, but he doesn't talk too much. He's smart, but he feels no need to be too demonstrative. He's broad-shouldered and glistening. He has this wonderful, wholesome attractiveness, with just a touch of a southern accent. Claude thinks in such absurd consequentialist abstracts that together we came up with a funny way of classifying our respective intellectual approaches: he thinks in projecting, capacious, and systematic abstractions with little relationship to what happens on the ground, and

I, focused on horizontal ethics, affect, and psychoanalysis, am feminized—doing, philosophically, *the housework*. Two nights later at the house in Île-St-Denis, I read and chat and play cards while Miles sweeps, collects dishes, picks up beers to share using money I give him. I love to look at the angel who works: shirtless, otherwise. I love quiet, contained, supposedly normative masculinity (when it tidies up the house).

Notes on the vocal, those for whom it clarifies and those it overwhelms: at the party in Montreuil, I met Miles at a stairwell in conversation with others. Hitting it off quickly, we followed each other through the house all night, finally in a room with Odile and her new romantic focus, who were dancing and having a more rambunctious time than we were. At a break in our conversation, we smiled at each other, and Miles asked plainly, "Do you want to make out?" Partial to such clarifications, I said, "Yeah!" and we found another room that was empty but for people's bags (an ethical conundrum—should we lock the door? No, our shame was worth less than the ability of others to access their belongings). Claude never asks: he kisses. During sex with Claude, which happened after an extended period of wordless pawing, I found actual penetration less energetic and forceful than I expected was his ability, so I said to him, "I want you to go as hard as you can." The language was plain and unaffected, but he came instantly, before even complying with the injunction.

He says, after (in his own defence? Of *men?*), "Sometimes the first time is fast." I don't think he is even aware of how funny it is that he, a straight man, should tell me with any authority how long it takes men to come. How many times have I first had sex with a man? I'm past counting. I tell Claude I have better access to this data than he does, but I spoil no secrets (the reality is obvious—every time is different!). I will not ever recover from how absurd I find Claude to be. Somehow still philosophical, he is the most closed thinker. Conversation with him is so *confined*, and while I don't quite think there's evil in his heart, there's just something that doesn't click. I told him the man whose house I stayed at in Île-St-Denis is likely in his program—he doesn't ask *who*, he just goes on to say that ENS has blah blah blah a world-class philosophy program. When I tell Austin of my friend, he asked, oh, I've probably met him—which one? I describe Claude, nondescript (uh—mid-twenties, small-medium build, white, brown-haired, handsome, *you think you know anyone like that? In your philosophy program?*). Austin does think they've meet, and Claude seemed "not to do well with people," which Lord on high is *true*. Where are all of Claude's friends? Why is all our time private? Why can't we be with others? He's been here for five months! When talking about past romantic vulnerability, I said to Claude, something of the last people I've been significantly attracted to relied on my desire to protect them, to give them something they were too debilitated to get from the world without my help. I saw discontented, socially helpless men and wanted to provide them the warmth necessary to see some light and welcoming in the world. It would make perfect sense that I should want to do the same with Claude, but there's something about him that so repulses me. I'm glad this week instead to be attracted to Miles, who appears comfortable with others, and structures his life on those bonds.

* * *

I have been made a coffee that is strange, spicy. It wasn't a desire of mine, but it's fine.

Very funny: last night, my first of two sleeping in Villejuif,

Odile slept in a bed with another friend, Ada, visiting from Brussels. Among Odile and the musical friends living in the house, Ada seemed, like me, quiet and out of place. This morning, we all lounged on laptops, synthesizers, guitars, and had coffee, listening to music and playing it. Around noon, Odile, Ada, and I took the metro up to Paris together. At Place d'Italie, Odile went in one direction and Ada and I in the other. Immediately, Ada confided: Odile never asks me *anything*. I told her, that's funny, me neither! Ada said that even though she thinks Odile is exhausting, she always ends up missing her once they're back in their own cities. I said, me too! But I don't even get exhausted, it's just that I have all these stresses in Toronto, and once I've flown over an ocean I don't want to relive them. I want a vacation from life and the company of a hyperactive woman always telegraphing her own stresses. Odile and I are joined, above all, by an aesthetic sensibility, visually and musically. She's better at both: a more creative dresser, a musician, a collector of records. But her choices are ones I *would* make. The music we were listening to in Villejuif suited this sensibility exactly: grainy, old, twinkly guitars. We are not reading the same things. Actually, there were few books in this house at all. My library resembles that of the communists in Île-St-Denis. But in many ways, the Villejuif house was the same as that one: welcoming, crowded; people in proximity living at their own pace. Different ways to draw bonds with others.

Rereading Agamben's *Highest Poverty*, which I bought when last here but never finished. In the monastery, you are not under the same law as in common life: you *elect*. You elect with a vow, your spoken belief and commitment is a subscription to a private set of ethics that you can't disavow without a withdrawal from your community. Like my new communist friends? Living to steal from the outside, sharing together, an ethic of non-dominance *within* the community. And a trust: that what they're doing is correct, that there is, abstractly, some *reason* for it. When in regular public life, your position has little bearing on your capacity to *believe* in something: you are ruled equally to your peers regardless. Miles and I spoke of meeting again, in August. I hope this happens. I'd like to know the people I met for years: the building, the praxis, but above all the kindness and invitation.

Actual poverty, the poverty of those without access to anything else, is more visible here than in Toronto. It makes sitting in cafés reading theory and writing reports on my inconsequential life seem incredibly facile. The standard of interpersonal ethics I seek is bourgeois. I have to accept that my thoughts of public intimacy and generous contracts stop just short of those with the most demonstrable need. So I've spent my time supposedly with activists who have some commitment outside themselves but think only of how it feels to socialize with them. So I want socialism, but live through a nihilistic compact with the world whereby I ignore the interests of anyone with less power than I have until I've somehow been made to feel satisfied in my own position. So I've accepted. So I've accepted that my present goal in life is to help other insufferable neurotics come up with new ways to describe their feelings. So I'm worthless otherwise. There are less admirable goals, I'm sure.

A final realization, of Claude: on only a couple of occasions did he say anything I agreed with, and they were probably just repeated from some book. He said of me, "You're all different sizes." So I've been told for a decade now. I hardly care anymore. My breasts, for their part, seem to have minds of their own, and plump up slightly when attention comes their way. It's OK that my life is still interpersonally precarious enough that it's apropos to ask, why don't I happen to desire *this* fucking idiot? (The asshole is such an idiot, fuck.)

On Claude and every emotionally debilitated, predatory fucker in life: they're *not rapists*, they just do not care whether or not the thing they're fucking would really rather be somewhere else.

I mean: I can think of Claude—patronizing, egotistical, evasive, selfish—as a *person*, or I can think of him as a beautiful failure of a masculinity that was just recently in favour, a signal of a better world to come. I'm not the only one who finds him repulsive: *this is why he's alone.* I choose optimism. Life!

OK, OK, OK, so there's adolescence, which is subjectivity as constitution by that *to which* you are subjected (oh no, I spend time with and have fucked someone I dislike and disrespect, like a person still searching for guidance from this world!), and then there's *adulthood*, which is being certain of your values, but knowing when you've chosen to compromise, because what we all want are better worlds than will ever be available to us (I have spent time with and fucked someone I dislike and disrespect, not because there was some truth there, nor because I had to, but because I chose to against other options [boredom, a public nap, the cold that would likely result therefrom], and it has neither changed me nor proven that I'm different from what I had thought before). I know this contradicts much of what I believe about a contiguity of desire, ethics, and action. But that, too, cannot be perfect in every case.

IT'S BEAUTIFUL HERE IN TOURS—A BIT BORING. BY THE TIME I leave, I will have figured out French, and I will have figured out life.

What turns on doesn't obey optimism or ethics. For my week on the couches of others, I did not masturbate. Within an hour of settling into my apartment in Tours, one can imagine my priorities. Though I've had some notion that I might stop watching porn in support of a future of orgasms conjured only from my mindscape, this abstract future did not concern me so much as my present orgasm, and I loaded up something familiar on the residence Wi-Fi, which is surprisingly not so bad. And, for the first time in a long time, I became distracted from the video by an image in my head—but *not* the image of the encounter I'd recently enjoyed more. I thought not of Miles but of Claude, because it was Claude who I had stared at. Though the encounter itself had made me feel unhappy and uncomfortable, I retained the visual stimulus of Claude's sustained suckle. I came not to the video, but to this, with my eyes closed! The experience of Claude was similar to my experience of porn: visual, disengaged, looking at someone *else's* desire from a distance. The suckle-face looks so great. I don't even know, when gazing upon them mid-suckle, if I understand them as my own tits. What I can change to come with others: open my eyes. As a reflex, I only keep them open when the other's eyes are closed, or when I feel, as I did with Claude, disengaged. But I only come with a visual! This unbelievable, overpowering shiver I always got from Oreste, this ineffable *feeling* that was never my own to generate: it was never the orgasm. It was just tension. And save for fleeting instances, my eyes were always closed.

* * *

Grand Marché *vide-greniers* was tight. Two silk shirts, Henri

Lefebvre's *Que sais-je?* on Marxism, and an old but untouched pack of cards, all for four euros.

OK, I found the *vide-greniers*, the *marché des fleurs*, the cheap café-bar with the good music, the philosophy booksellers, the record store, the Lebanese sandwich places, and now the café where the Marxists are. The music is not good here as there is only so much to share.

Who am I in touch with? Some chatting with Ivan, who says he has a long email coming; with Max, who feels immobile because his father has fallen ill again; with Freida, who injured her back; with my roommate, who doesn't yet know if he's moving to NYC in September; with my mother, who's still only feeling so-so. Short emails with Miles. Most recently I sent him my Fourier lecture and some of the more romantic passages from *À nos amis*. Haven't written Odile since getting to Tours.

* * *

OK, Tours is great. The language institute is ideal. Classes are terrific. There must be a few hundred international students all combined, but only fifteen students per class. The professors are kind, bright, and clear. The students are competent and confident. I'm the oldest, but not by too much: most people are between nineteen and twenty-two. The campus is pretty, small, just three buildings around a square in close proximity to anywhere I should want to go. The Institut is lovely. It makes me feel, *surtout*, awake.

I missed a trip to Amboise with the class group last night because I felt sick to my stomach in the morning, but had I only forced myself, I would have had a better day. I expected that not having had a day to myself since my arrival in France, I really *needed* one—but, choosing to spend the day in my flat, this didn't feel true. Without habituating oneself to the pattern of solitude, there's nothing to find within it. I spent time on Facebook again, but I wasn't rapt, I was bored. I played solitaire, but it didn't pull me into a spiralling time void. I was giving myself medicine I didn't need. I masturbated maybe four, five times. But did I need to? These lonesome orgasms will not change my life. They will not even speed it up.

* * *

Altogether, what there might be to dislike about the Institut is that I'm only here for three weeks longer. It's been lovely. It's been a kind of language instruction I've never gotten before: conversational and engaging, never by rote, giving us the material we ought to respond to. I still speak slowly and shyly, with constant unease and a consistent stammer, but it's coming. It's just so enjoyable! Each day, my comprehension improves. My verbal recall, too! Today we had our first in-class exercise that will be marked, and while I worry about my orthography and my preposition use, which is just a matter of practice, I didn't feel that what I *wanted* to say surpassed what I was *able* to say. That was a terrific feeling.

A month might be the perfect amount of time to spend in this place where I do not *quite* have friends, but I am friend*ly* with everyone, and I like my daily routines very much (back at the apartment: cook nice meals for myself, as I hadn't done in Toronto, attend to only my own physical organization, do daily calisthenics).

It has happened: there's no one in my mind to whom my thoughts are directed. I feel free and unbound. Hopeful. I have to remember when I next obsess myself with someone or something or some purpose not to forget the feeling I have now. It is one of pure potential. It is the only way I feel neither mania nor depression. The question is how to return here when I next inevitably depart. The answer seems to be: give yourself to a new task, something discrete from your previous life, or leave Toronto, or *really bar yourself* from those things that cause you anxiety. (It doesn't suffice not to contact Oreste—you must neither contact nor monitor him. It doesn't suffice to leave it at Oreste—you mustn't contact nor monitor Helena, either, and still not Julian.) And right now, there's no one else in all the world who makes me feel as though I could be compromised, who makes my stomach sink. Only three people in all the fucking world cause my stomach to sink! Plus: I'm vibrant and still young. We're not under law, we're under grace, motherfuckers.

* * *

I'm in Paris again, for the evening, where Odile plays her last show before recording her album in Berlin. It is hot, hot, fucking hot here, and not in Toronto, which is unusual. Paris is especially magnificent when you've been cleansed for a week by a small town.

On ceding to one's desires to quit the abbey and return to Paris: there must be a model of remaining single with close proximity to intimacies, which is close to the image of someone who cannot bear to be alone in the countryside, who rushes to the bosom of the city for the same feeling: lonesomeness with an out.

* * *

I *think harceler* means *to molest*, but according to this book, monks only got six months in prison for doing it to children, so maybe it means *to teach a shitty thing to* or *to trick out of money*.

Show was fun; I slept with Alexandre, the best-looking and sweetest one in *that* group. Everyone I've slept with since arriving here is so young and so *handsome*. Alexandre is twenty-three and fucks like he is. He's so, so cute. Such a well-structured face, beautiful, beautiful thick, curly black hair, kept short. Also: *very kind*. We took an incredibly strange journey from the 11th to the 6th to the 14th arrondissement to Villejuif, and I saw the largest and most beautiful apartment I'd seen yet in Paris, which belongs to Alexandre's mother. He grew up where the rich grew up. Plus: the best-looking person in most rooms. It is completely to my surprise that he seemed untrained in fucking, or perhaps we were not physically compatible. I am slutty since arriving. I have always used protection. I stepped accidentally on the condom after I'd put on my clean socks this morning. Imagine that, after sex, you had to? That it was mandatory to step on the condom.

* * *

Feel still lovely. Got back into Tours last night on the final train from Paris. Alexandre woke up early to move a couch from his mother's, which he had promised her, and I didn't stay too long in Villejuif, worried that if I were still asleep in his bed upon his return, I'd have worn out my welcome. Slightly hungover, but mostly dehydrated from the heat wave lasting over a week now. My slightly dispassionate account of last night does not do justice to how lovely Alexandre is or how refreshing he is to spend time with. He's not a difficult person. He plays the guitar for Odile (the house in Villejuif, as well as the default bed-and-breakfast for friends-of-friends from out of town, is where they practise). During the show two nights ago, he looked handsome playing. And he told me, well before we kissed, I looked rather good dancing. I had a considerably nicer experience two nights ago than just "fucking the cute one."

They played another show last night in Barbès, and I had plans to meet Odile there to drop off the phone she lent me before heading back to the train. They played early enough that I'd be able to watch before heading back to Gare d'Austerlitz, but I wasn't really up to hanging out again, and purposefully waited until the last moment to go. Said hello to Alexandre, and Odile, and everyone, because I've somehow developed an air of familiarity with many. Alexandre apologized for the hectic night and quick morning and said he had a seven-hour disaster with the couch. Odile left with me and we waited together for my train. She had finally made it clear to Anton that she was ending things with him the afternoon prior, and we talked about that, and her developing feelings for Bruno, and the conversation, which I'd initially felt too shy for, was lovely. Now that I'm witness to more, now that I have my own connection with those Odile talks about, I don't feel so alienated. I'm thankful for her passion. At some moment on the metro ride, actually, it began to overwhelm me how much I owe to Odile, how magnanimous she is to me, and the extent to which she, alone, has made Paris into a sort of second home for me. She felt *supernatural* to me—the concerts, the friends, the warmth, the freedom, a whole network of others, familiarity I hadn't felt in *six months* of living in France the first time. Behind it all, this creative, passionate woman. She adored to hear that I'd slept with Alexandre, that I'd chosen "the good one." Bruno, her object of attraction, is a very bizarre man and perhaps a disaster. He is scattered and flirtatious and self-deprecating and in need of saving. But he's exciting, and perhaps a little manic-seeming, and supposedly quite good at playing the drums. Bruno reminds me of Julian, a *lot*. Odile recognizes all of this. She says, no matter what happens, she's not worried she'll be hurt, because he's sensitive the way a teenager is, and she's so much stronger than him! I said, I don't know about this: when you come to care for someone, it doesn't matter if you can recognize that they are like children in their emotional development—worse, it can make you want to lose confidence, kindness, and the capacity for emotional articulation, just for the chance at being right for them. She says, oh boy, I know this is true. And then for both of us there is this feeling of congratulation that I had been attracted to Alexandre, whom she knows well and has only the kindest things to say about. Life is not a straight line; neither is your desire. But sometimes desire can behave with a sensible, forgiving maturity.

Of French and of life: when I fail to understand something, it's most likely that I've come in with the expectation that I'd hear something else, and I'm not open to anything but the simple binary of correspondence/non-correspondence.

* * *

I think I have been suffering from hypertension, but I'm just going to breathe more deeply, and stop eating kebab and drinking more than three coffees a day, and I won't freak out about it. Since I've been here, it has hurt my heart to do push-ups, and this morning it exhausted me to walk to school, too.

Sometimes French words come to me first. Being at the Institut is effective. I wish the course were six weeks long (it's four). I've been planning vaguely with Miles to go down to the south to some big party at a *chantier* in Tarn, but I think it'd be better not to exert myself so much until I feel my circulation and breathing have returned to normal. This stuff worries me. Never felt tension in my chest before this year. I do not want to reach some position of calm, centred adulthood and then immediately develop a heart condition, Lord.

I think, due to how slowly I process sound in French, I don't develop memories of speech very easily. I can never remember what anyone says to me, and further still, I can hardly remember what I say to anyone. Some utterance just gets forced out in haste while my mind is equally preoccupied with producing a better phrase than I could, and soon after I have no recollection of what it was I *did* say. This could also be a way to avoid forming memories in one's mother tongue.

Sometimes, rather than being unable to remember *what* was said, I simply can't remember in what language. Last Friday, wandering the streets back to Villejuif with Alexandre, I misused a qualifier, *beaucoup* instead of *tout*. He corrected me, saying, "People don't say that. *I* like it, but people don't say that." I don't know whether he said this to me in English or French. I registered it in the language most comfortable to me, because I thought it was a great thing to be told.

* * *

Watched a documentary on French communists at the Institut's *médiatheque* that clarified that the pre-'68 French communists were emotionally useless. They were just Stalinists! Their social values were hugely heteronormative in order to preserve familial order so as to produce more communists— as one woman said, three children for every family: one to replace the father, one to replace the mother, and one for the party. It was a program of shared wealth and labour with no imagination for art or pleasure. And when the students came out in the streets that spring, the party had *no idea* what was going on, and no interest in joining it.

I chose against going down to the Tarn to party with Miles and gang since I am still waiting until I feel no symptoms of hypertension. Did I just fall back out of shape having forgotten what it feels like to be out of shape? Plenty of people tire instantly climbing stairs (right?!). I visited a little typography museum (which was just a small printing house with a room of ephemera) and the Pierre de Fenoÿl exhibit at the Jeu de Paume arm in the Château de Tours. Both lovely.

*   *   *

Strange thing: my physical condition has worsened. I can't even say when this began, this strange pressure I feel daily upon my heart, the new limits I have to impose upon my physical exertion. This morning, I had a little heart seizure before leaving for class. It was incredibly painful and arresting, so I finally visited my program assistants to tell them, and they made me a doctor's appointment for tomorrow morning. I don't know what's going on but I'm certain it's not in my head. And of course there have been *so many false ailments* that I've been certain of having during my life. But this one: I'm really sure. Something is up.

All the same, I feel fine. Never like I'm dying. Not worried even if I have to change my diet or take medication. Not worried in general. Actually, the whole ordeal slows me down. I breathe more slowly; I'm careful not to get too excited: I think it's *better* for my emotional state, and for my concentration, to have a slightly tired heart. The extent to which I am without general worry makes me feel certain my brain is not conspiring with my heart against me. My roommate told me he is leaving the apartment to NYC, blessed be, and Max offered himself up the empty room in September. I have nothing more to do or plan and I'm happy with it. My chest still hurts.

Lord, try to explain to a medical professional how strange it is that you were once an anxious person, but now you're so calm, so how could it happen that *now* you're having possibly life-threatening heart problems? Explain it with a straight face, in French. I was told my blood pressure is excellent and my heart beats only as quickly as that of any worried person. The pressure I feel on my heart when I move my upper body in certain ways is the pressure felt by people with overstimulated hearts trapped in tiny rib cages. So I've been prescribed an anxiolytic the doctor recommends I take for three weeks, whether I feel anxious or not, because it will bring my heart rate back down to normal, where nothing will hurt any longer. I'm not dying of heart trouble. Maybe for months in Toronto I had been inadvertently taking an anxiolytic and it was called marijuana.

* * *

Still feel disheartened that I can't leave behind my conscious worries without them just making their way to my subconscious, speeding my heart up, as though something I'm not even feeding still gives them a reason to continue on. This is foolish. My life is on *vacation*, and little concerns me here. My bank account is replete with government-borrowed funds. I have a single responsibility and nothing else to worry about. Class is enjoyable and instructive. Further, I don't miss home.

I don't know what the problem is. I did, after taking the anxiolytic, sleep incredibly well last night.

I can never tell if it's the drugs that make me feel different or if there's never a day that I don't feel different. Either the drugs have calmed me in a way I wasn't aware I needed to be calmed, or I was ready to feel some way and call it drugs. Anyway, drowsy yesterday but not today, but I feel slow today, in a good way. It's not like Cipralex, which made me feel dopey and impotent. It's that I'm *slower*. I can think of all the same things, there's just a lot of noise I don't have time for anymore. This is a good way to be saturated.

I rush past: feeling secure; the right language; everything. Notable that one of the things I took to indicate my heart failure was that suddenly I felt the exhaustion caused by walking at twice the pace of everyone else.

Oh, *will*: I am feeling somewhat lacking in *will*—but not like a depressive. In life, my will has most often taken the form of a will *against* something. I am willed back to my apartment or toward something vague and unavailable. This is the kind of will that ultimately does little more than make me perpetually uncomfortable. This is the will I am presently lacking.

* * *

I like to read and dream about fully conceived, fully formulated utopias: I fantasize that if I submit myself to some regime I suit well enough, that regime will surreptitiously become inescapable. It would slip under my skin and I would eventually lose any thought of retreating from it. The order it would give me would fix my life. It's the same fantasy I have when beginning relationships—that if I fit well enough with someone,

I'll begin to belong to him, and if only I were to give someone more of a chance, belonging to his order would fix my life, so much that I wouldn't be able to remember any desire for a life outside of him. But: I know too much. I wasn't born into any of it. I'm doomed to live sharing with, not living in. (Except: this isn't doom. This is freedom when it's accepted.)

Wandering attention threatens she who worries that she could be under scrutiny. Fixed attention does not. Many in proximity with focused attention are no threat to one another. You are permitted to focus your own attention at will when you are forgiven from asking, finally, "What should I be doing?" I've arrived at the Centre for Expanded Research. There is no surveillance in the library here, but still it retains its function: in this room people are concerned only with their own work. There are no cautions in place to ensure that books won't be damaged or stolen, so the collection is fluid and materials are lost. They will be replaced with new materials.

Insofar as CER has administrators, one of the administrators has a baby. The baby is friendly, trusting, and a joy to play with. Sometimes the mother leaves the room, but the child always has self-appointed company.

Ruby told me there are three rules here: "Leave no traces"; "Make it possible for others"; "Do or decide." I said, I don't really understand the distinction. She said, no, *The doer decides.*

When listening to a speech about the potential for social change through erotic praxis next to the more handsome of the men here for the week, *and* there is a baby in the room, I feel like praxis isn't possible, because I just feel flush.

* * *

Two nights at CER so far. It's more wonderful here than I could have anticipated. I feel no social anxiety around the group. A seminar is on for the week. All food and drink is provided and prepared. We eat together, we participate in seminars together, we can meditate together in the chapel each morning if we so choose. It's luxurious. The facility, a converted monastery in rural northeast France, is what I'd imagined a Phalanx might look like. Rooms of different sizes, high ceilings, music rooms, libraries, several kitchens, spaces for quiet, and spaces for noise. When you want to organize something for the group, you write it on the chalkboard, and people may participate at their will. There are collaborative writing and discussion seminars. One scholar had us in groups devising shared definitions of the erotic, and what I discovered was that people can be very territorial about their definition of the erotic. There was surprisingly great tension around this. Ruby doesn't give priority to speaking with me before other members of the group, which is fine. Haven't been writing much, but read the *New Yorker* yesterday, like, front to back. Big earthquake, big catastrophe imminent. People here are very verbal. I sleep well. My bedroom is cute, with a comfortable spring mattress and a view of a tree-lined hillside. Something in the scent of the sheets reminds me of vacations to New England as a little kid. I think. They give me a cottage feeling, one of being suspended in time and looked after by others.

* * *

I'm not certain I find this seminar intellectually rigorous, but it is calming. When the historian leads discussion, I like where it goes. When the poet leads discussion, or meditation, I like that I feel physically at ease. There's a certain aspect of the poet's methodology that seems foolish to me, or at least not fully thought through. They seize upon one form of pleasure—creativity!—and theorize life around it, as though all it should take someone to enjoy their life is to be better in touch with their creative faculties. I just think this person has a much better considered approach to pleasure than they do to misery, which has equal power in structuring our lives. I do as much to direct my misery as I do to direct my pleasure, and it's clear to me that writing each day does not make it so I am not miserable. Aiming to produce art only invites into your life a host of new miseries you'd never have known of otherwise. Why is the world at the office rather than here with us at the commune? Not strictly because others are being forced, but because not everyone considers the choice we have made to be desirable. The valorizing of creativity for creativity's sake seems vacuously therapeutic. How can one ensure that creativity-for-creativity—creativity-for-*health*— doesn't turn into an empty form of therapy separate from their life? It just seems like in seminar there's a whole lot of idle talk about how *this* is the way to live, and that if everyone else were "in touch with themselves," there would be no more greed and no more poverty. Not that people organize their lives upon innumerable pleasures and stresses, and it isn't somehow the right choice to make poetry or whatever we're doing here.

In any case, I love the commune. My rules aren't the same here. If I'm chilly or if I'm kept up hearing my neighbours make love through paper-thin walls (the detail with which I hear the sex is astonishing—down to the suction of the kisses and the very gentlest, normally inaudible sighs of abandon), I'm not really bothered. Discomfort doesn't accumulate in my body as stress here. All flows through. Because the space isn't mine, and I feel grateful to it. I don't feel I have dominion over it.

Finally spent alone time with Ruby yesterday, which was lovely. Took a walk together before lunch through the pastures and the woods, and after dinner and a couple glasses of wine, took a bath together in a sumptuous wing of the building I hadn't seen. It's easy to speak honestly with her.

* * *

Last night I slept with someone primarily due to our shared capacity for extreme misery, but you cannot give up absolutely that which brings you closest to who you are. I can never forget how joyful it makes me to share misery with another. I laugh more. Hangovers too are a special and distinct experience of being and I feel more *alive* during them than sometimes otherwise. Mutual rejection (of the rest of the world) is hugely intimate. I feel great this morning after Noah, whom I didn't have to share a bed with because mine was just down the hall. You say to another: creativity doesn't solve misery and we cannot seize upon the generation of it like it's the antidote to a bad life, and he's like *yes* because he knows, obviously; he's just finished his PhD! On Kant? I tell him I've never even considered giving a shit about Kant, but it's cool. I ask him, is it conservative to prefer some people to others? It's so important to laugh, Jesus Christ. I am having a hard time identifying with others at the commune, but he insists it's not a commune because there's no duty, there's will. Not under law but grace! My enjoyment of and engagement with everything in life is so heightened when I have been laughing. Who gives two shits about permissive public touch. Laughter is the shit that's joy, man! Like, the difference between putting music on because silence feels vaguely bad and being chained in place unable to take your morning constitutional because each song queued up is *the perfect song* that you had *completely* forgotten about while the previous song—which then seemed like *the song*—was playing; but here it is: the true song, and it's fucking very good. The difference between those experiences is joy! Of anyone I've fucked since leaving Toronto, I've been the least physically attracted to Noah, but fucking him has made me happiest. He told me I was beautiful enough that earlier he'd had to resist staring, and I was like, right! Such statements are a part of this thing. This deal. The fuck deal.

*　*　*

"Thought is a moment of solitude," someone said during one of the seminars, and I agree. It's been a very special week at the residency, but I didn't get what I thought I'd get out of it. I never found the seminars totally enthralling so I participated in only half of them. It is a place that operates under an ethic of freedom, but nevertheless I have a stifled feeling to be so close to a group of others I feel the pressure to be present for. We've all elected to be here. We've all nominated ourselves as each other's contemporaries as open, creative people. Supposed intimacy is immediate: it doesn't have to be won. I feel guilt when I just don't want to be around, when I'm just not interested in something. I don't think I'm very clearheaded when there's an ethic of pure communicability. I don't want to share all my thoughts! I want to fortify them in private. I articulated with Noah that I think I'm at the point where I'm really splitting open what social anxiety means to me. Guilt has sometimes pressured me into claiming anxiety when, in fact, it's often that I choose against things. I reject things, and I don't want to take responsibility for that choice. You get more sympathy from suffering than you do by rejecting.

It's not as though I've *disliked* this week—I've just reached limits whereafter I want to be elsewhere. I don't know how it should be that I, so *intellectually* interested in public intimacy, should want it only by piecemeal when it's right there to be indulged in.

Slept with Noah again last night. We were near each other at dinner, had some wine with Ruby, and then split off to be by ourselves—I asked him to show me the unfinished and uninhabitable wings of the building. I have splinters in my palm from feeling my way under the wooden beams in the dark. I get along with Noah, but I don't know if I would have initiated sex if he hadn't. I feel unattached to the idea. How I felt yesterday, giddy upon the cultivation of joy from twin miseries, it was just: *right*, I'm familiar. I know exactly what is happening and exactly what proceeds to happen if you consecrate the object with whom you share your distaste for the world. You become vulnerable to it. I can tell Noah anything, and I kind of *do*—that I've never had a relationship lasting more than a few months, that I have hugely stilted and erratic attachment patterns, that I think I have a way of understanding and practising devotion that is different from 99% of the world. That I've never come with a partner. That I have a weird interest in mommy porn. If he's hard or not because he has intimacy issues, too, I don't care at all. I have to explain to him that if I laugh during penetration, it's a good sign. He likes being a bit dominant and testing the limits of dominance, but after I say no when he pulls my hair, he doesn't do it again. Again last night I suggested we not share a bed for sleeping. He seems like an honest person, like when he confesses to being nervous or says he's always amazed when women are interested in him, and I wonder, is this what men are thinking? How barely I'm attached to its outcome lets me be free in sex and more selfish than usual, or at least not impatient to rush past cunnilingus to something that will stimulate Noah's dick. No, I will not tap his shoulder and invite him up; he shall stay there as long as he sees appropriate. I don't know when sex last felt like it did last night: sensationally good but ultimately unimportant. I don't have any investment in how he should behave with me the morning that follows. I feel warmth toward him; I know what warmth feels like; his degree of comfort or wish to fuck me again are not issues I'm anxious to uncover. It's nice to fuck him, and he's interesting, good to talk to, but I have no concern whatsoever with how he feels about me or what he might want from me. If this is what freedom feels like, it's as safe as it is bland.

* * *

I have now left CER. I am joining standard public life by way of the café across from the train station, which is broadcasting horse racing, a locally beloved sport. I have a different way of being attentive to life when there is a possibility of threat. This is necessary for my attention. That everything at the residency gets taken care of, and no one trespasses on your space or on your person, everything's so respectful and safe, I don't know. My surveillance faculties spend this time sleeping. Everything was comfortable, but I'm glad to go back to the world I have to be awake to. I like both worlds. I'm glad to have had the opportunity to circulate between both worlds.

Another friend of Odile, Paz, wrote to offer me a sublet in the 20th, so I'll be staying there instead of Villejuif. Alexandre, to whom I hadn't spoken in a month, texted me yesterday to say he had left Paris for holidays but had hidden his keys somewhere so I could grab them if I needed a place to sleep. I would be disappointed if he were gone the whole time and I didn't get to see him again. All the same. It was sweet that he offered me his keys buried in the sand.

* * *

I'm worried about spending time with Odile and her friends tonight, starting from what feels like scratch again. I'm glad that with Noah I found a cynic at the commune to be intimate with, but I don't think he'll leave the impression on me that either Alexandre or Miles have, because they represent activity and newness to me and Noah represents: the life of a man finishing his dissertation. It's like: I know. *I know.* It doesn't make me dream of the glittering possibilities of earth.

It was nice, though. As I was listening to music and writing an email (to Ivan, among other things, *about* Noah), he drifted into my bedroom and we chatted for a bit before I invited him to hang out and work, so we lay in my bed listening to piano songs as he read about Kant and I read about Spinoza, one of his hands stroking my leg and hip. He slid his fingers under my shorts and began to jerk me off while we both kept reading, and when he slid off my shorts to eat me out, he invited me to continue on reading if I wanted. Though I did find the idea of this a little sexy, I didn't think it sexier than rude, even with his permission. So I placed the book to my side and had my part in the cunnilingus, sighing. We'd fucked the two previous nights and I didn't have so much of the fuck energy left—yesterday, possessed of an odd sort of serenity, I didn't have much energy at all. Just as well I didn't feel much pressure to bring myself to energy's occasion, so everything proceeded slowly: lying close; long, firm caresses. He finally fucked me on my side slowly and deeply, but not for long, either because he was more excited, hadn't masturbated recently, or, for the first of the times we'd slept together, hadn't had anything to drink. I take passive pleasure in fucking and touching slowly. It feels good like it's just feeling good *to* me, because when the excitement and pleasure generates from *within* me, I always tend to move fast. His hands, which never stop moving on me, just make me feel empathetic: sometimes I too am possessed of the unstoppable urge to explore. Not on Noah. It's like my mind already makes up that I want some other body, so I don't play around with him.

First class between Reims and Paris cost less than a euro more than the alternative, and despite my political belongings, I am luxuriating.

I nearly began crying on Noah's chest yesterday afternoon. After he came, I lay beside him, tapping my fingers lightly on his shoulder, staring at his chest. I wasn't upset, and I wasn't miserable, so I don't know why I started to tear up. Soft music streaming from my laptop. The feeling of passive pleasure that didn't produce excitement or exhilaration. The suspicion that I'm entering a stage in life in which this is the kind of experience that will dominate. Like my wish for years has been to experience sexual pleasure without the vulnerability that it has usually relied on, and I've been granted that wish, but I fear I've unknowingly offered up the opposite experience in exchange for it. If I never miss Noah, if I never fantasize about sex with him again—did I still enjoy the way his dick felt inside me? *Yes.* And that shit can make you cry if the music's right.

OH, THIS IS FUNNY. A FACT I'VE HEARD A FEW TIMES this summer, but never earlier, is that Thoreau, writing in his cabin about a purity of self through autonomy and isolation, was actually right down the street from his mother, who regularly brought him meals.

I'm learning to be open; I'm developing into a woman who can actually be turned on by another person rather than having to do the psychic work herself before they arrive. To *not* have to be good to go. This is not settling or accepting less. It's adapting to the speed at which others move. It is slowing down and getting in step with people. It's less risky, because you learn to take pleasure in *others*, not in some projection of your private world onto the body of another that you can't *see* because you spend all your time with your eyes closed to avoid learning what he's actually like. Because you do not want to know how little he resembles you, or how little you desire to resemble those parts of him you're blind to. To go more slowly is to take the time to be attentive to the touch of another—to feel slower pulses of touch as they move through you, exciting, failing to excite, always producing some or another sensation. You go too quickly and all you feel is the life being knocked out of you. ("I don't know *what* happened, but it was terrific!")

Autonomy is the funniest notion. This week I'm paying for an empty apartment, and I feel a freedom I couldn't have felt when staying with friends. Now I have a place of my own to come and go from as I please, because I met Paz through Odile, because I went out to concerts, because I've been warm with people who've been warm with me. Every link contingent on some earlier link. But look at me, I'm autonomous now!

Just dreamt of writing to Helena, I don't even know if I was joking, "I'm not sure of the quality of the last email I wrote you. I am really trying to keep myself at the edge of language."

* * *

Serology report used as bookmark of book borrowed from shelf of my sublet: little could be more intimate.

Odile came to sleep over last night after a show. Sleeping next to her, oddly, I dreamt that the proprietor of the arts residency had died in a skiing accident, and the group of long-stayers (including Noah) were forming plans to split the estate between themselves. I then dreamt that I slept with a professor who behaved in the style of Noah, slipping off my track shorts to go down on me, but he was married and it was a very big deal. Learned from Odile that Alexandre, already in the south of France, won't be back in Paris before I leave, and she thinks it's sad, too. She hasn't seen her friends much since recording with them in Berlin, so last night, hanging out with her and the others, was nice. Miles comes into town today. You really do not become obsessed by singular objects when open to whichever are near. Autonomy. Being in Paz's room is nice because she is a musician with a certain sensibility. Her bookshelf is like mine but smaller; her windowsill is decorated with plants. Her roommate, Alain, throws parties, including the concert I went to my second night in France. He's throwing one in Lisbon I might go to while I'm there.

Dancing is a ritual I believe in. It's sensible to live floating without preference between whomever or whatever should propose itself to you. I feel great. Not sped even slightly but totally great.

From Paz's shelf, Ian Svenonius (in the "Sex" chapter):

> Since these ideals of womanhood looked like they were sixteen, mid-60s girls attempted to look—and act—like infants. Thus, when the groupies appeared, they weren't actually sexy or sexual. [...] Groupies weren't interested in sex. Their sexuality was incidental—they had the erotic sophistication of bonobo monkeys. Eros for them was a transaction, a means to an end in a world where a female's only asset was her willingness to utilize her sexuality.

> As with modern DIY "indie" music, and "amateur" pornography, groupie-ism was more about power and narcissism—using the tools that were values by the power structure. The assertion of self was the point of the transaction, similar to the one in which the majority of the bands were involved as well.

A funny thing about last week's seminars: the insistence that just the word *erotic* should be ours—it should be rescued, pried from the hands of those who use it for evil and dominance and put to use by the utopians who want to maximize positive sensuality. But why not just use *sensuality* instead? Or *amity*? Eros has always involved violence. Let the powerful have it. (What's the trouble in leaving erotics to the fuckers?)

It's a bit absurd to talk of some purified *true* sexuality unmediated by *representations* of sexuality and plays of power. It felt during the seminars as though my sexuality didn't even qualify, because it's too insecure, too sprawling, too infantile. It's insecure, it's sprawling, it's infantile, and it's real. It's *mine.*

How can the same mind made tired and paranoid by life under patriarchal capitalism still so desire it and be unable to take pleasure in the ease of the commune, an environment of acceptance and permission? (Acceptance has its limits: how well can the other accept that I do not accept them?)

One reason people tend not to free themselves from the imposed direction of external standards: it's not in anyone else's interest, so others are unlikely to advise you to do so.

The historian, at the residency, pointed out the obvious emphasis on feminine beauty through cultivated smallness and weakness, women seeking to develop explicitly less healthy bodies in order to suit the sensibilities of a dominating aesthetic. I thought of my body hair, and how much I can't help but despise it, though it too indicates that I have a healthy body. Though I don't have a weak body, and I love my body for its thickness, the particular details of the thickness I'm happy with still meet a normative feminine standard. Small but soft, dominable yet bountiful, and white, white, white, with the endless privilege extended by these qualities.

Here's the way I dominate the sphere of attention: I wear very little clothing in cities in the summer. It's not "work," so the attention doesn't feel like a reward, and it doesn't feel ethically right.

* * *

To me, Miles's politics seem simplistic though stable, and

hardly involve desire or misery or affect at all. Structurally solid: *one should build shared autonomous spaces; one should engage in crime.* Whereas I wonder: why are we all bound to that which we *do*, and what if one enjoys living in the city, reading sentimental philosophy, having lots of alone time, playing cards with their friends, involving themselves minimally in the larger capitalist economy except for the purchase of food and residential rents? I don't think his praxis has the patience to account for the extreme valences of human desire or the possibility of living an engaged, satisfying life without totally absenting oneself from the public world. I don't know that his understanding of feminism or anything more largely comprising "identity politics" (as he calls it) is terribly nuanced. I got angry at him last night when he called the 20th a shitty neighbourhood and I was like, what the fuck, man! Nearly told him to go home but then felt like, no, I could still have sex with him. Miles's healthy, healthy body so fascinates me. He's no theorist. He has such a gorgeous physique. I don't feel when I'm with him like I'm discovering my own ideas or having them opened up. I sometimes feel like I'm translating those ideas for someone in a different register. I get annoyed, but then just look at him! He's so *strong*. It makes it so I want to fuck him but I still become bored when fucking has commenced, and penetration becomes painful before he finishes. Then I think about Oreste, and what he said to me shortly before we stopped seeing each other: that he couldn't stop thinking of what I was like when I fucked other people. And I told him that mostly I stop enjoying penetration much more quickly than with him. During sex with Miles, I don't feel intimate with him; I feel separate. He went down on me for the first time (when we'd first slept together, I was menstruating), and I got distracted when an embarrassing song came up on my computer. Sex with him is not an experience of dissolution. But then just look at him! He's so muscled and golden and healthy all summer on construction sites and communes and farms. Realistically, he knows how to do all sorts of shit I don't know how to do. He told me some comrades were *building a plane*. This afternoon he stole a Simone Weil book for me but then told me he didn't think there was any such thing as subversive living without literally criminal practices. Is this so? He told me how often Roman got into fights, and it made me suspect that much of their praxis is just hooliganism. Hooliganism's not a program, but I think it's kind of sexy he stole a book for me. I told him, not only is criminality unimportant to me, but the commune is not something in my plans. And further, as a woman, what I think is ethically important is mostly to claim intellectual space and resist the domination of others in order to maintain my autonomy and will, to be a more effective feminine subject than would have been possible a generation ago. I think, had this been Noah, I could have joked with him: ultimately the goal of my feminist praxis is to achieve orgasm in the presence of another, and we'll see about the rest thereafter. I didn't feel, the way Miles engaged with me, that he would be able to see that I was saying this in jest as a veil over total seriousness, because pleasure and presence *are* praxis, man! Would I be able to come in the commune if there were no big capitalist world outside it? We can't speculate. To speculate is all we can do. The way Miles talked about his longest relationship and smaller involvements since made it sound like he enjoys being in a couple, but feels a political injunction to resist it, so he resists. This is so strange to me, this *submission* of one's desires to the supposed spoils of ideological prescription. I tell him: I've never put politics before my sex life. The way I want the world organized is dependent *upon* my desires (or, if my desires are under ideological influence—and they are, certainly—the influence is deep enough that I *feel* the desire before denying it over a political injunction). If I desired to be with anyone exclusively, long-term, I just *would*. They'd have to desire it, too, of course. (Ideology is too safe deep in my libido, like a little burrowed bug.)

Lack of real pleasure will attract one to the weakest sort of liberalism. *For the time being.*

* * *

I guess the question of (my) life is, how do I not simply endure, but bring something of each experience into myself? I won't go without *metabolizing* each day as though I can somehow convert even the inedible into nutrients. It's a way to insist on memory, and to insist on autonomy. So, this summer, which is properly *weird*, wherein I don't feel particularly intimate with others, I write constantly and translate each experience back to and for myself later, because I don't feel I have the best opportunities to process it and share it with whomever makes the most sense (Caroline, Maurice). I'm not even writing long, intimate emails (to Helena, to Ivan). I guess it's that I haven't been carrying on a single therapeutic relationship.

Spent yesterday with Ruby and a friend from the residency, Trevor. Dropped off their things at my apartment after their train ride into the city and took them on a nice walk from the deep 20th to the Yiddish cultural centre in Chateau d'Eau, via the cemetery (Ruby loves cemeteries!). Mind certainly was active at the time but I don't know what to make note of. When Ruby mentions Helena, I experience jealousy, but it's just an experience. I know why I have it. I know it troubles me that Helena's relationship to Ruby is one of greater intellectual curiosity, one in which it has never occurred to her to pimp the girl out to her brother. I know that it makes me feel jealous to hear that Helena has recently emailed Ruby out of the blue whereas she and I haven't spoken in months, and it makes me *feel as though* Ruby has somehow remained more useful to her, or that Ruby holds her respect or interest better. Jealousy tells me only of my own insecurities. It doesn't tell me otherwise of myself, or of Helena, or of Ruby.

There is something disquieting about the *capacity* to turn away. The last two nights in the 20th, I slept somewhat fitfully alone. I'd slept more calmly beside Miles and Odile the two nights prior. No sleeps better than at CER, where, though alone on the mattress, I could not choose whom I'd be eating breakfast with, and who (Ruby, Noah) might wander into my room. (I desire choice, but realistically I prefer being surrounded.)

Dictum: allow yourself the experience of passion, abandon, but never so much that you forget to pee afterward.

Ruby's friend, yesterday: continually anxious about the idea that we didn't know where we were going, though he couldn't have had any real concern for where that was, because he didn't have any stake in it. Still very important to him that wherever it was we were going, we didn't lose our way. I found this anxiety annoying because I'm in the process of battling it in myself. (I suspect that this summer I've made some very good progress.)

Simone Weil, providing counsel I could have used months ago:

> A rock in our path. To hurl ourselves upon this rock as though after a certain intensity of desire had been reached it could not exist anymore. Or else to re-

treat as though we ourselves did not exist. Desire contains something of the absolute and if it fails (once its energy is used up) the absolute is transferred to the obstacle. This produces the state of mind of the defected, the depressed.

To accept the fact that they are other than the creatures of our imagination is to imitate the renunciation of God.

Affliction in itself is not enough for the attainment of total detachment. Unconsoled affliction is necessary. There must be no consolation—no apparent consolation. Ineffable consolation then comes down.

It's possible that the body lags behind the mind, which is no explicit shame.

As I was saying about sex with Noah: "As soon as we know something is real, we can no longer be attached to it."

Just straight up crying on the metro for no reason but indiscernible existential anguish and possibly a lapsed anxiolytic prescription rn!

* * *

Yesterday it wasn't purely existential confusion that caused me to cry on the subway. When I chatted with Max, he confessed that he would "probably be using the apartment more as an office" and sleeping primarily at Cybil's. I said this was nothing surprising and nothing to worry about, and that he could only upset me by pulling out at the last minute and leaving me no time to find someone for the room. He said he wasn't planning on this. He wants to be close to family, and I am family. At the end of it, I have probably had more contact with Max since I've been abroad than with anyone else. Much of it is just updating the other on our emotional states: "I feel sad/excited/strange/etc. I can or cannot think." His choice about the fall makes little sense to me: why he should, if involved in a relationship, choose to stay in an apartment with another woman with whom he shares such affection. I have no narcissism feeding upon the situation, and no feeling that I'd like to monopolize his affections, and no feeling like: oh, though I know very well it's best we stay supportive of each other, why isn't he too sexually attracted to me to involve himself in this? I feel fine. So why did I cry? I don't know. Affection is beautiful.

There is no way for someone to tell if the conversation I shared with them served a therapeutic purpose for me. (There is no way for someone to tell if the sex we shared served an intimate or recreational purpose.) In either case, they'll be able to venture a guess.

Whomever should produce himself at my side is the one of my preference. I am now ready for death. (Joking, joking.)

It's just unsettling the extent to which, though I don't feel like God has been with me, I feel like Simone Weil has:

> Attention is bound up with desire. Not with the will but with desire—or, more exactly, consent. We liberate energy in ourselves, but it constantly reattaches itself. How are we to liberate it entirely? We have to desire that it should be done in us—to desire it truly—simply to desire it, not to try to accomplish

it. For every attempt in that direction is vain and has to be paid dearly for. In such a work all that I call "I" has to be passive. Attention alone—the attention which is so full that the "I" disappears—is required of me. I have to deprive all that I call "I" of the light of my attention and turn it on to that which cannot be conceived.

I turned down hanging out with Claude to hang out with Miles, and turned down hanging out with Miles to be alone, because sometimes all that isn't therapeutic is exhausting.

Perhaps foundational, demoded psychoanalysis and contemporary fashionable feminism share a method: of uncovering some original, primary wound, which, if resolved, would allow you a clear pathway to remake yourself? Is there some way to do this without conferring with whomever it was that wounded you? Is there some way not to demand an apology? Is there some way not to hold resentment? Radical forgiveness is not much advocated for women insofar as all we've ever done is forgive.

Statistically, young women lead the change of language, which means I should be able to write as I please, but on average, women are speaking *with* each other, and not always making such bizarre departures.

* * *

When living here a few years ago, the attention I received on the street made me feel sick, weak, and beholden. Now it makes me feel kind of powerful. I don't feel as though someone's speech gives them any licence to me. I just feel like, well, it's good, yes? Most men are not forceful: they just make a little comment and move on. The few men who have followed me or berated me for failing to dignify them with a response, I've been very comfortable just yelling at and moving on from. Hundreds of comments and not a single man has touched my person. Again: I *do not wish* to be an apologist for this stuff, which attracts such ire, and I know that a little younger, I really was hurt by it, really felt as though I owed something, either shame or attention, to the men who spoke to me uninvited. But now? I don't know. It feels like another form of public intimacy. I like the way I look and how it moves in the world, and when men are like "*ravissante,*" "*charmante,*" "*manifique,*" when it ends there? I *like* it. Before I didn't like it. The problem from a public-ethics perspective is that it's no one's responsibility to like it. Also, before, most of these men, mid-to-late-twenties, still felt like my elders. Now they are my peers, and in some cases I'm older than the men who call at me. I just don't feel like the weak one anymore. I don't feel like because someone's announced that they can see me I have some responsibility to them. It's summer and I feel fluid: does it make much of a difference that someone should call a stranger beautiful rather than just smile at them? (I know it's all still shitty for those women who, like I once did, feel fear, responsibility, and embarrassment, but I've really come around to it.)

What happens when you come around to a world that isn't good to you? Take your pleasures where you can. Or renounce them as perverse, because when the better world dawns, there will be better pleasures, too.

* * *

Little dinner party at friends of Odile yesterday. Smoked some hash. I'm not doing much research to ensure that my time is most imaginatively spent here and, were I weaker, I could get upset with myself for this. But instead my largely unvaried days are not disappointing me. I do whatever I want, which lately consists of having intensely emotional days strolling, thinking. Will see Miles tonight. On the thirteenth, he flies to the States, and Odile takes the train to the south. Lucky that I leave the fourteenth.

I stole one copy of the *Que sais-je?* on Freud and another on the Popular Front, not because I couldn't or didn't want to spend four euros, but simply because I didn't want to be a hypocrite who wouldn't steal for myself but would happily have another do so on my behalf. I now have no reason to steal again.

* * *

I think that most of what Miles says makes no sense whatsoever, but I have simply never *seen* a body like his (nude, up close). I wish it weren't rude to ask to take a picture of him.

His sex drive surpasses mine, though I consider myself to be the less good-looking of the two of us (most bodies do not make me feel like mine, in comparison, is doughy and malformed). But the key to a stronger sex drive for me would be if I were to find him funny, or if I were to find him to make sense more often. He has many large ideas. Many large, untethered ideas (about the revolution).

In any case we'd both find ourselves agreeing with Simone Weil when she says: "After the collapse of our civilization there must be one of two things: either the whole of it will perish like the ancient civilizations, or it will adapt itself to a decentralized world."

But maybe I alone can agree further: "You could not be born at a better time than the present, when we have lost everything."

Yesterday, while it was still light out and I wasn't yet eager to fuck Miles, I asked him, "Do you think there's some relationship between periods of hyperactivity and anxiety and your sex drive?" He said, "Maybe, do you?" I said, "Sure, absolutely." And he, "So, you're telling me you feel calm right now?" Yes, quite calm indeed.

* * *

Woke with vague and physically pressing feeling of unease this morning but stayed slowly and calmly with it, identifying its components, coming to the understanding that nothing that contributes right now to a feeling that I am stuck is so bad.

I finally got a rejection from the Toronto lit mag to which I sent my story in June, which was particularly discouraging because one of the editors had been at my reading. But also: not a problem. Simply something that didn't happen.

It's a blessing that I should be sensitive enough to the physical manifestations of frustration and anguish that I can feel its onset as a pressing, a closing in of walls, or a caving in. This is the narrative my subconscious is establishing: because some things in life do not go forth without friction, I am trapped. But as I can feel this narrative as it's being drawn up, I can stop it with close attention: there's no trapping. There's leaping out of events that won't be of any further consequence as I disengage from them, and there's the understanding that what's easiest for me is not what's easiest for someone else, so I resign myself to a new path of action somewhere toward the centre of the two desires. Then the anxiety lifts.

I feel right now as I always feel at the beginning of August: sweaty, stuffed, and ready for fall (I have not left for Portugal yet. There is a-whole-nother seaport to this odyssey).

Funny, my twin standards for intelligibility: when I don't make any sense to people, they're simple, impatient, inflexible, and uncreative. If Miles doesn't make any sense to me, he's talking out of his ass (language is never perfect).

* * *

Julian favourited a tweet of mine last night. Can we continue on? No matter how I feel or what I do in life, I still feel somehow like I am a thing made for his tastes beyond all others. He will always be the one who knows how funny I am, or how funny it's my intention to be. And all the rest of the world will continue to make the mistake that I am serious or sentimental or sexy.

* * *

I like Miles more each time I see him. A certain resistance has been a part of this. When I'm hanging out with him and his friends on the canal and saying I want to spend the night alone because I think if we fuck right now I'll develop a UTI, he says, we can still spend the night together. I say, I'd prefer not to, and he doesn't push it, but by the time I get back to my place, I wish we had. Part of this was accepting a ride home from a stranger on a motorcycle who then took me to the other end of the city, and while he stopped in to a convenience store to buy booze, I fucking BOLTED, and then told Miles that there's only such a thing as a free ride from comrades. I have now employed the term *comrades* fully in earnest, like him, and he says, that whole ordeal sounds terrible!

Yesterday at the canal was someone who had been patriated to France because he helped facilitate the escape of a French prisoner who'd been captured by ISIS. Remarkable! I never stop telling Miles how he looks to me. Healthy and big. Like the Americans deployed to World War II who completely awed their skinny and deficient European counterparts. He said he'd never been called a doughboy before. Remarkable! I said, impossible, you are *such* a doughboy. I'd planned initially: Tuesday night with Miles, Wednesday with Odile, but then just because I wanted to, I told him, regardless of what I do with Odile tomorrow, I'll spend the night with you after, in Paris or up in Île-St-Denis. To date easily for two weeks is ideal.

Helped Odile move. Montreuil again. I love going through her things, and I love being with others on significant days and the feeling of peacefulness that comes with it. The best way I know how to live is by suggestion and invitation. Did I email the editor I saw at my reading when I was drunk last night to ask what the matter was? Yes. Will I follow up if he doesn't write me? No! Does it matter: not at all.

I'll miss the music played here out of cars and in bars. I'm ready to go but I'll miss everything. It's unreal that I feel no anxiety to fuck my terribly handsome lover, but I look forward to *hanging out* with him and the *Appelistes* before spending the night with his arm around me. Had it been Alexandre, would I have felt just the same? So many lives are suitable. The one I've fallen under especially. Remember, two weeks ago, I was at the monastery, with another? Everyone is foolish and summer is sweet. There's really no one to seek counsel from, because there's no one who knows better.

* * *

Must one steal from the margins in order to begin altering the basis of the structure? (Capitalism, love.)

I read too slowly and my friends are gone. Odile is a legitimately magical woman with inexpressible powers. Miles left the bed I'm in an hour ago, and it feels gloomy. Maybe it's not kind to explain to someone that they've never once made you nervous and it's one of the reasons that summer's been so great. I didn't sleep well but I had a dream about Max. Max and I fucking in some apartment resembling the one I just moved Odile out of in Montreuil that I'll never see again. But more psychedelic. What does any of it mean? Leaving Montreuil yesterday evening toward Île-St-Denis, I was grateful not to be heading back down to the 20th. The house in Île-St-Denis is lovely if dirty. Nice courtyard, books lying all around. I'm not sure what everyone does here, but their shelves are replete. Ate dinner with Miles, Eli, who lives here, and two new Americans. The new guests and I shared a sense of humour. Better than Miles and I. But Miles and I share an enthusiasm for having sex with each other and sleeping while touching. He got hard fewer times this night than the last one he spent at my house, so this time I was the one who wanted more. I'm welcome in New Orleans, but perhaps I won't be if he's seeing anyone. I'll be welcome either way. But in one case we most likely won't be fucking.

The adjustment to an island of family for two weeks will be difficult. Odile told me there is a party in Lisbon that is likely to be wild, and people will probably be taking drugs should I so desire, and I believe I should. Are any of us really sticking the wrench in capitalism? Must radical contingency nauseate me so? I really could have given anyone a blow job my second night in Paris. Anyone could still have been around for another blow job my second-to-last morning. They never face-fuck you the first time but they might later, especially if they've a plane to catch. Miles wouldn't tell me what he wanted from me when he thought about it, but I said, that's fine. I said I have an incredibly thin membrane between my desires and my speech, but it's not this way for everyone: "Some have many membranes all scraping up against each other." What am I ever talking about. We talked about taking plane rides and that being at the airport makes him nervous. I said, every time I'm in a plane, I'm ready to accept death, and I don't even want to consider that if it were to crash, I might survive. He says, but people *do* survive! Begins to explain to me how to preserve your body as a plane falls. I go, please, I have never wanted to hear anything less.

Miles, last night, told me he didn't think I was energetic; he thought it was likely very important to me to put the effort forth to be present for others. *Thank you.*

Dark, from the copy of *Theory of the Young-Girl* on Paz's shelf:

> The Young-Girl would be the being who no longer has any relation to herself *except as a value*, and whose every activity, in every detail, is directed to self-valorization. At each moment, she affirms herself as the *sovereign subject* of her power, all of the crushing assurance of this flattened being, woven exclusively by conventions, codes, and representations fleetingly in effect, all the authority that the least of her gestures indicates, all of this is imme-

diately indexed to her *absolute transparency* to "society." Precisely because of her nothingness, each of her judgments carries the imperative weight of the entire social order, *and she knows it*.

There's no better relationship than any relationship before its first putrefaction by renunciation. There's nothing like the easy early purity before having to reaffirm what you earlier renounced in order to fuck again and everything that comes with all *that*. One thing I'll never know, because Miles *was* here this summer, is how lonely, anxious, and far from myself I might have felt if he hadn't been. If I do miss Miles in the next couple of weeks, it'll be owed primarily to having so little to occupy me in the Açores.

The editor I contacted *did* write to give me generic advice about rejection, and it was very kind. I told him I just wanted to be the one people trusted better than themselves, whom they considered wise, who set the standard of dominant style by my own work. Part of the advice (which he excused as patronizing) was, if I wanted to be published specifically at this magazine, I should read it and aim to resemble what it looked like. All this contemporary short fiction aims to make a barely altered life look either enviable or precious, and I can't in good faith aim to do the same. My barely altered life must look just as it is: unremarkable, deniable. It cannot be presented as *precious*. There's no mystery to whatever choice. They are each as easy to make as any other. Readers prefer description to theory. We all do what we can. I want to skip the step where I aim to resemble others so others can resemble me instead (in person, at least, friends tell me my way of speaking is infectious; but not all of them tell me this).

Extreme ambivalence strengthens attachment, which has to be renewed upon an assent each time it's renounced. Equal disposition to whatever should pass with a loved one allows for a relationship of total tranquility.

But further, remember: with all intellectual flourishes neutralized as simply cutesy-quirky, all under God are available to be boyfriends!

The extreme transparency of a seemingly comprehensible place makes radical contingency seem less threatening, or less real. I don't think of Toronto this way. I don't think of all the other lives I'd be living on a single decision alone. I feel I can see everything, and can therefore see what in everything doesn't suit me. I foolishly believe that "no matter what," I would have come to know my friends in Toronto at some time or another. As Paris is opaque to me, I can't comprehend all those other lives and niches, so I know they are multiple, and I have ended up with the particular makeup of my own life due only to luck.

The real tragedy of Toronto: we don't own anything. We constantly have to move our things around between "lucky-find" apartments to keep up with the market. We have to give up all property to strangers, not our own community, in order to have the freedom to move our bodies around. The house in Île-St-Denis is owned; another, full of comrades, is owned just down the road; and by next month a group of them will be purchasing their third. You can't own anything in Toronto, and neither can your friends. Your best hope is a storage locker, which will probably end up relocating somewhere where the rent is cheaper, too.

Self-interest is but the apparent motive of the Young-Girl's behaviour. In the act of selling herself, she is trying to acquit herself of herself, or at least have them acquit her. But this never happens.

* * *

The most idiotic, privileged, childish anxiety: *"Will I continue to want this?"* If you're in a good mood, probably!

It's not true that I am equally disposed to any outcome with Miles. I'd prefer that he come to visit me in October, and maybe we take the weekend to visit comrades in Montreal, and then I go down to visit him during winter break. And, who knows: maybe everyone comes back to France next summer. I know he wants to. I think I'll apply to teach in a high school in France through a program advertised in the French department each year. And then I could spend the summer here again. There is so much available to do.

The thing that has to happen is that all my friends go in on a property where we can leave our books and mattresses and cook dinner together, and everyone is invited. And we make our own wine because it's cheaper, and my grandparents can teach me. I know, I know. The demands of school are going to subject me to an experience of anxiety again, but it needn't be significant. I feel calm and able. I feel like if I had a partner or security or any money, I'd be ready to have a kid. (One sees so many kids in France, and they're energetic, social, and sweet. I see so few kids in Toronto, and they're so often these little shits. I trust that in time this desire will leave me.)

It's true, and apocalyptic, that I think that to reproduce my life (have a child), I have to give up my life (take a job I don't want, maybe a partner I don't want, too, re-establish lines of contact with members of my family I don't want to know, move somewhere difficult to access in order to have more space). In Toronto, it's difficult to see any other reality as true. But, all over, there are different opportunities, different possible lives. I love coming to realize, each year, how much I want to raise a child. It makes me feel big and loving, like these breasts have some purpose more noble than vanity after all.

When I believe that my own exceptionalism is the only way I'll *be able to live*, of course I'll fling between episodes of depression and mania, of course I'll suspect myself of being perpetually unable to measure up to standards I seek out from every figure and institution. If I believe a full and pleasurable life is available regardless of how well I'm able to *distinguish myself*, then there's less to propel me toward these emotionally debilitating states of being. You just work. You just continue. You fill your life with friendship. Everything's good.

I'll be approaching the Spanish border in minutes, and the Portuguese border in hours. I see palm trees and mountains now. *Salut.*

Family

IT'S PERFECT THAT MY FAMILY REALLY DO LIVE ON AND come from an island all their own. Metaphorically perfect. Narratively perfect. I never know what *literally* means in contemporary language, but in that respect probably perfect, too.

Crashed last night. Exhausted, private, hungry feeling. Some hours walking through Lisbon but many more in the room I rented. Thought about 9/11 while plucking out pubic hair. We need these nights. You cannot reproach yourself for giving yourself these nights. I'm on a plane now leaving the European continent. On the Açores I would like to: jog every day, swim every day, eat plenty of fish, and translate Barthes on Fourier. In an hour I will be in my grandparents' care. I have a tickle in my throat. No one could eat all the garlic and pepper in Pico.

* * *

Heavy rainfall and minimal construction has actually encouraged *more plant life* on Pico now than when I was last here. The air is perfect, though it smells occasionally like animal shit (if you're near it). Figs larger and juicier than I've ever seen them. A problem Jameson writes about: if you achieve utopia, you might lose its spirit. It's true that in Pico, there are minimal aesthetic and intellectual traditions. Who needs them. All anyone here dreamt of was acquiring some capital elsewhere to bring back to weatherproof their homes, and they did it. Everyone eats well, and while the men normally have manual jobs that work it off, the women are normally a bit fat. People are not habituated to shamefully eating snack foods in private. At least not during the summer, that I've witnessed.

People here leave signs on their gardens, or near trees, saying, "Come eat." Very Edenic. I took a picture of one such basket and a man came out of his house to chastise me for taking a picture instead of a tomato. And so I did take a tomato, and it was good.

*   *   *

To concern oneself first with the emotional and affective is still true philosophy. Loving better is the practical imperative of the hour. The inability to take others into our care is a primary fault of anyone I know, myself included. In the Açores, everyone knows how to welcome others, but oddly enough no one knows philosophy. Emotional enfeeblement is as bad as not knowing how a home is put together.

*   *   *

I've started to dream of Oreste again in the mornings. I know it isn't really dreaming of him, the real man with his qualities. I'm just dreaming of sex again. I'm just cleansed of attachments, dreaming of the last body to present me with not just sex, but dissolution. All the ways I've been with bodies have presented the spectrum of what I know as sexual, but at the end of the tunnel is still dissolution. More sublime than sexual, containing sexuality in the abstract. So, when days or weeks or months have passed and I've forgotten relationships and bodies and people, my mind wanders toward the pure feeling of sexual dissolution, a memory of which is still produced with Oreste's body as a sort of re-enactment hologram. Time will keep passing, and the vision of dissolution will continue to grow more abstract, and eventually it'll have no face. I'll just sleep in and have a *feeling*. It won't remind me of anyone, not even abstractly. In that moment I'll finally be present and free.

Five Fs of securing lodgings: friendship, fucking, financial capital, family, political association?

* * *

Extremely calm trip each day together with family, nourished well and not thinking too much. And they certainly don't either. Really it is my grandfather who is living the dream of wandering attention. His mind is like a vine: shallow and growing laterally between anything directly before him. But he's kind! And he can build a fucking house. I'm never really alone here, but my grandmother is careful to give me space for something close to solitude. So careful, careful even to clean up after me and cook for me and do my laundry. Each physical need is taken care of such that it will be an adjustment to be responsible for myself again. It doesn't suit me totally to be on a shared rhythm: at lunch, I eat when I am not yet hungry, and by the time dinner comes, I feel ravenous and eat too much. Constant socializing is a difficult demand. If I am to offer myself some way I'd prefer to do so in the kitchen, which I'm barred from so my grandmother may attend to all tasks with private precision. On the whole, I eat too much because every meal is followed by bread, cheese and fruit, and fruit brandy. I have sometimes been eating just at dinner what in Toronto would last me all day. So has everyone else! I'm walking lots, swimming, getting lots of sun. I feel healthy if plumping up slightly, and I'm very relieved that I'll be leaving all this extreme generosity and leisure in five days. Yesterday, took a ferry to the island opposite ours and toured around it my grandparents, my great-aunt and uncle, and two second cousins. Both boys, Rafael, a teen, and Laudalino, twenty. Laudalino was the tour guide due to a gentle sexism that suits me because I benefit a great deal from being treated as a child here. That my mother's cousins are younger than me perfectly fits in the strange age arrangement of the whole family: my parents ought to be my siblings, and my grandparents, spritely, are of an appropriate age to be my parents.

In Faial, we visited the museum erected near the ruins of the town where my paternal grandmother was born, which was destroyed by a volcano in the fifties. When I last visited the site—when I was a child—you could still see the remains of many houses half-buried in the sand. Now you can see almost nothing, and healthy greenery grows from the sandy deposits that blanket the former town. In under twenty years, you can do more than double the work of the forty years preceding them.

Laudalino and Rafael are closer to me genetically than anyone but my parents, because their mother is from my mom's side and their dad from my father's. Their father, my paternal grandfather's first cousin, suffers from a depression that is either unusual on the islands or not often spoken of. My grandfather died early, of heart failure, a condition that accompanied a divergent psychology whose particulars I've mostly pieced together from others—a complex arrangement of symptoms and expressions summarized, insufficiently, as psychosis. My paternal grandmother's hometown was *destroyed by a volcano* when she was a little girl. My grand*father*'s parents, a woman from Pico and a travelling labourer from the continent, died when my grandfather was too young to make a memory of them, from tuberculosis. He was raised by two of his aunts who are old but still living and who I've seen this week. My paternal grandmother, after the volcano, immigrated to Connecticut, not Canada, during the fifties, where she first landed as a refugee. She'd never met my grandfather until he, after immigrating to Toronto sometime in the mid-sixties, travelled to Connecticut on business (my dad said he designed and sold clothing? I mostly remember that he went to the hospital and wrote political pamphlets for distribution around our neighbourhood). My grandfather decided they were in love so he brought her back to Toronto to be married, and during the seventies they had three children: my father first, another son, a daughter, each dealing with some health problem first experienced by my grandfather. During his marriage to my grandmother, my grandfather was physically and mentally abusive and his multiple hospitalizations were against his will. At some point, my grandmother left him and took her kids to her parents' house in Connecticut, but then something happened, I don't know, and she came back to Toronto never to leave again, and not to remarry after my grandfather's death.

Mother's side: my maternal grandfather is from Pico; both his parents are as well. He is an elder-middle child of over ten kids. He has never had anxiety, depression, or psychosis. He is of a social and generous disposition, and not a controlling one. My maternal grandmother's parents are from Pico, too, but she was raised until seven by her grandmother on the other side of the island for a reason that has never been made clear to me, and she doesn't have any siblings. She is of a more nervous disposition than my grandfather, but it's nothing like the other side of my family. The two have an equitable relationship. They came to Toronto in the early seventies, when my mother was just a year old, and my grandmother was pregnant with a second child, a boy, who passed of crib death at three months. Two years later they had another child, my aunt, and no more. They were nervous and protective of my mother and aunt, who grew up in circumstances my grandparents distrusted and did not understand.

My mother and father had always known each other, both their families from the islands now living in Toronto. They started to date as teenagers. My mother became pregnant with me shortly after her sixteenth birthday. She confessed it to my father, who proceeded to tell his own father without her consent. My father's father then bullied my mother's parents into an arrangement by which they would be married. They first attempted to live together in an apartment downtown, but in destitution, they were moved into my father's parents' home.

My father was mentally and possibly physically abusive with my mother. My mother wanted to leave with me at five, but something happened (the next year, her father-in-law died). We left when I was ten. And then, when I was sixteen, she left me, in order to move to California with a new husband, to an apartment downtown I could barely afford. I was horrified that some circumstance would force me to move back to my childhood home. I immediately began a sexual relationship with someone I looked up to like a father, who was mentally abusive. I was constantly worried that I would become pregnant, and felt furious when I would instead get some physical ailment (UTI) as a substitute for the punishment of pregnancy. And then the rest of life.

My paternal-paternal great-uncle from this trip has recently been hospitalized, due to his nervous disposition, though he's spent his whole life here in Pico, and never suffered the trauma of migration between two distinct worlds. There's the perspective that he's sick with what's in the family blood, and then there's the perspective that it's not the blood, that he too has some trauma bounced off from some trauma bounced off from some trauma, stories I don't even know of connected in some way to the premature death of his aunt and her husband, or to the behaviour of his grandparents.

The best gift I got in childhood was being left alone by a bunch of unfinished people too focused on their own problems. And so I got some space in the world. The best gift I was given was the void. The freedom to live without boundedness is the freedom that presents me with the bulk of my anxiety at present, but it is a *gift*. It's the chance that I can break out of the skipping stone of trauma and somehow not continue to pass it down to children and lovers. Like Weil: from the void, from emptiness, you accept grace. You detach. You can still *love* while being detached (I'm having a very nice time here!). But you love others in their separateness, in their real being. You do not consecrate histories simply because they were given to you. There violence lies. From grace, and from detachment, you accept that you cannot repair violence or do justice to what you've witnessed by bringing it upon another. There is no justice. You separate yourself. You separate yourself from a duty to what came before you, and you start anew.

(Or how can it be that one is still depressed, living only so barely under capitalism? *Shit's fucking fucked, man!*)

It takes little more than the comically literal repetition of trauma (ages, figures) to demonstrate that it's not only chance; it really is *devotion*. If we were less bent upon re-enacting circumstances to which we've already been subjected, it would at least look *somewhat* different the second time.

* * *

My grandmother, this week, described the conditions of her poverty upon arriving to Toronto: cramped apartment (*check*) in the west end of Toronto (*check*) on the third floor, sweltering hot, with no air conditioning (*check, check, check*), decorated with furniture taken in from the street (*check*). She describes it with the same impassioned feeling that she gets describing the poverty she left in Pico (no plumbing, electricity, or preservation of foods). She describes it as though these two states are near equal, only states to depart from. Whereas I see my mild poverty as tolerable, shared, and *almost* meaningful.

If the hysteric is, at her core, she who searches endlessly for truth, and the master is he who is not concerned with truth—he simply desires that everything *work*—my maternal grandpa, who does not like discussing emotional or figurative things, but desires that people behave or pretend to behave decently to each other of their own accord (and who so fittingly made his profession as a carpenter), is a master. Maybe the only master in my familial lineage.

Also apropos this flourishing recount, as though a volcano museum was my madeleine, the tour starts with a neat 3-D movie about the volcano, which, pursuant to it being a geological phenomenon, starts *at the beginning of the universe.*

Again, a logic of enduring consent applicable in depression: if this weren't how one had to live, I'd never agree to it.

*　*　*

I feel guilt over my separation from some members of my family because I can't identify the problem perfectly: it isn't clear to me. It is a mark of having been witness to the abuse of another and perpetually feeling proximate to it.

The idea that trauma has to surpass some limit is built into its definition as Freud delivered it: the *traumatic* wound is the one that pierces. The trouble is that no two people will ever have the same threshold. Extreme diversity in this, even within families, in generations woven tightly as fifteen or twenty years apart—between my mother and I, between her and her parents. A world of precarity and changing rhythm will provoke traumas in some and not in others, and the near immeasurability of what registers as trauma requires that to understand what is traumatic—or even undesirable—for another, we exercise radical trust and love.

The anxiety of each misstep proving to your family what they assume because they want you closer: you are not fit to live. The fear of asking for help because you can't risk that this be revealed, because you suspect it of yourself. The fear of asking for help because they don't know how to help, and they've no interest in learning: they simply want to pull you back in.

*　*　*

I thought my grandmother, at home in Toronto, did not like plants because they're too messy, but I discovered here that she loves plants, and that all the ones in her house in Toronto are plastic only because she spends all summer in Portugal and there'd be no one to water them. And then I remember: *right*. The office above the woodshop where I spent my afternoons with her as a little kid was a fucking jungle. This could be why I like them so much.

I suppose I got exactly what I wanted this summer, which was to have a mind that could direct itself to whatever I should put before it, and not to long for something distant and invisible. I no longer feel preoccupied or dissatisfied. As far as the Açores, I prefer to be with my grandparents when my mother isn't around, and with my mother when my grandparents aren't around. They're all much more pleasant without what the other brings out in them. No emotional matter worries me. Of course I should feel good: it is still summer and I am not in school yet and I am not back in Toronto, where sociality is the Açores turned on its head: here, everyone welcomes you for nothing (or: for family) and it takes no social work or charm. There, it is a constant game of charming and beguiling in order to gain entry, the off chance of being welcome if someone happens not to feel guarded that week. Then you guard yourself accordingly. You're all of you miserable alone at home preparing yourself to be impressive enough to go out and see someone again, next week. Cultural producer's ethic cultivated from work and taken into the home, into sociality. But I'll live with someone I like. And I'll be at school all the time. I'll smoke a nice lavender joint every Saturday after work with some fruit liquor I bring home as a souvenir. And perhaps, in a year, I'll leave again, to somewhere I like better.

* * *

Stupidity is the quick skip. It comes from supervalent thought concerning a stable imaginary object or, otherwise, the enduring conviction that thought isn't worth your time (the first manifestation I have suffered; the second is prevalent here in Pico).

That I might be able to demonstrate to the world that I am effective, like an insecure child. I've sought this through sex. I must somehow know only joy and never the anxiety felt upon the injunction to impress someone. It should be so easy to see that attracting someone to you has no relation to how *effective* you are, despite my adolescent path toward confounding the two.

If women have finally uncovered, honestly, that to love men we need to pity them, and men have finally discovered, honestly, that to love women they have to dominate us, how is heterosexual love at all feasible? We'd need to return to being unsure of these matters (or: we'd need to give them up).

* * *

Slept quite poorly over the past two nights. I don't know if it's the surfeit of thoughts I've had during the day in comparison to the week prior, or the pressure system (rain and wind that have mostly kept me in the house having thoughts in the first place). I have a throat ache that worsens each night, a constant, low one that I carried over from Paris. Suspicion has me ascribing it to being throat-fucked by Miles the morning he left, which I don't even like, but there were no condoms left and I thought I should make him come. Was one of the reasons I suffered no anxiety with Miles because I cared so little about the sex, or at least about my own experience of pleasure? I mean: I wanted to feel good, but I wanted more frequently to just give him an orgasm and then look at his body or fall asleep. Or I just wanted to hang out. I just wanted to hang out with the person it made sense to hang out with, to whom I grew gradually attached through the act of hanging out. The sex didn't feel integral, or the focus wasn't on sex for me, so I never instructed him to do what I like better, and I didn't protest when he fucked the back of my throat before he caught his plane. I don't know. I have a throat ache because people get them, in particular those spending months with no fixed address. What does one gain by only fucking when they want to fuck *the most*? They gain either falling in love with someone who'll do something about it or giving themselves a reason to feel very sad.

Oh! I dreamt so much last night. New transformations of Pico: the mountain, the roads, the coast. Another was a sex dream I think made me come but there weren't really any characters and I can't explain the contours of it.

Love, the event, and the family. What the young do now is postpone all these things. But they simply form new social groupings that reproduce the worst of the family, without any of the security and with fewer of the benefits. Some such groupings (Île-Saint-Denis, friends from high school) retain more of the benefits. The models built upon shared aspiration toward creative production are most often terrible, eruptive, insecure, put too much in peril through jealousies and competition; again, *everyone* wants to dominate the landscape of attention.

Enduring anxiety postponed: how will I ever be so compatible with a man that I should have a child by him, and also have the means to support it, before turning forty? Everything seems impossible until it happens. In any other case, your imagination is doing useless work, tricking you with something false.

Saw a dog in the back of a moving truck, attached by the throat on a leash to the car: the beginning of thought, but not the end of it.

* * *

As I prepare to return to Toronto, I do not feel as vibrant and open to possibility as I did leaving it. I rather feel a closing. My family in Pico feel like a fully extrinsic *amenity* to me. I feel privileged to *have them there* for the chance to be witness to that world, but the bulk of it has little to do with me. It's horrible to witness the closest thing I might to truly communal, agrarian life, and no one has any intellectual conversation whatsoever. No imaginative inclination! Everything is just: who lives where and who is related to who and what happened to them.

Very common word in Portuguese: *ficar, to be located/placed*. The verb is the depth of many statements: direct your attention to that: it is there. This, too, is closing, and makes me feel like in the last two weeks I've gotten little more than *rest*. But it's not rest that really energizes, it's stimulation.

Last night my grandparents had the uncles, aunts, and cousins over for dinner, and after everyone left, I couldn't sleep at all. Juiced two hours of sleep from the night before waking up to prepare for my flight. I'm spoiled to have such generous, open family members and never tire of thinking, *But I just wish they had something interesting to say!* I don't know. I have half the appetite of these people when it comes to food or luxury. All I want are some good books and conversation (but the sunshine, figs, and ocean water certainly didn't hurt). Different appetites. Is this wrong?

These are people who've never had anything but company all their lives. They know pain, care, and hard work but they do not know solitude and they do not know its value. The trouble with family: it is *not* bare proximity, it's invested proximity. It's immobilizing. It made me so anxious to do any number of regular, daily tasks in view of my grandparents so eager to believe I can't do anything (so they might do it for me instead). Like this, too, with language: treated as this poor thing that can't speak Portuguese because they only speak it *around* me, never to me, so I can't understand anyone else speak, and so I can honour this inability, as though I'll just arrive there one year, having learned to speak it somewhere *else*? So finally I just ask them to speak it to me when the language is simple. It is bizarre to insist, "Don't infantilize me!" while accepting the charity of others. But that is what charity must be: a gift you choose to give out of kindness, not a contract with the fact that another can't take care of themselves.

I liked the weeks for swimming and eating and plants and animals. It's a wonderful place to be. It's not like the seventies: young people are not anxious to leave. Now that there's plumbing, weatherproof homes, and the internet, they don't need North America, or even continental Portugal, for very much. For the returned boomers, it must have been that the North American capital brought something else along. That the ethic of communality was interrupted by an injection of foreign money and all its attendant materialism. The homes rebuilt by expats resemble suburban North York mini-mansions: manicured gardens full of semi-tropical plants, with taller, wild versions of the same species looming over from the next hill.

Bizarre that just as I should articulate my distaste for what occurs in the domestic/familial realm, I think of making my own (I have never had so many daydreams of pregnancy and early motherhood as I have this summer). More than once, I've thought: if I somehow were the recipient of a whole bunch of money allowing me rent and nourishment while completing a PhD, I would get pregnant *yesterday*. I want the domestic warmth I can invent myself completely on my own terms, at least until the child develops its own subjectivity. I want to plump up with something half-mine that I can give, upon delivery, what I've always been taught is a contradiction: protection together with freedom. I'd enact through my own kid what I want to prove to myself is real. I'd be occupied with a completely new light on the world. All the love I'd give it, I'd receive. Ideally. It's not so strange that one should fantasize in this way of doubling the self. The species depends on it. The species depends on at least once having the fantasy of increasing love by doubling the self, and then acting on it.

Everything's so easy to fantasize about when you live with those distant and dissimilar from you. In hours I land in Toronto, but I fear it: to live again with many whose sensibilities resemble mine closely enough that our friendships don't *work*, because all it brings out is friction.

Anyway. You can read into whomever whatever incapability and mal-intent you want, but ultimately you have only yourself to forgive: for wanting to be elsewhere, not wanting to listen to people talk about where things are, how much they cost, and who they are related to. From the window, I see Canada. Life begins again.

Love

SINCE RETURNING TO TORONTO, I HAVEN'T BEEN getting much sleep, but I feel good. The night I arrived I felt a tinge of need for Ivan after coming home to an empty apartment, and tried calling him, but he wasn't around, and Max got home before Ivan returned my call. I attended an interview reading Freida performed, and Helena was there, and we didn't talk. I wrote her a short, friendly email, which she promptly returned with one of her own. Why did neither of us say hello to the other? Because *people are very uncomfortable*, and we are all liable to assume that someone wants nothing to do with us. On the whole, lately, I haven't felt like this. I've felt light and receptive, because this needn't change now that I'm home. It's foolish to idealize Paris as though my experience was of some permanent, unchanging community. There are fragmenting attachments and discomfort everywhere. You build the closest thing to the life you want wherever you happen to be.

It all feels about equally pleasant. Been back to the library; seen many friends. Long walks, circumstances, running into people, being thankful for the chance to get to talk to them. Things aren't uncomplicated with Max, but so far I love living with him. We're extremely sweet with each other. The standard of kindness is high. We kiss a little but I won't have sex with him because I have no interest in doing so. I've gotten no time to feel lonely, and if I'm lucky I won't for months. Maurice and Rebecca are on the west coast right now, but they'll be home soon, and then euchre.

* * *

What inspires my sexual response isn't always generous, and it isn't always kind, but at least it's complicated. What if what inspires theirs is simply that I look a little humiliated?

Chatting with Max is lovely, but this will not turn out well. Finally, I feel exhausted, but I am not able to sleep in. I'm over trying to find some motive for my sexual desire or my lack of it. I relate to Max in a very particular way: sentimentally, intimately, comfortably. Dare I say near lovingly. And *physically*: I am drawn to him, and I love cuddling with him, kissing a little, being held. But these things don't feel to me like the sexual that is genital. The moment Max gets *turned on*, I feel like, this again!? And then I feel embarrassed and guilty because I brought it that far and I feel beholden to him: and we keep doing this, *every single night*. We've had a few really phenomenal conversations since I've been back, about sex and relationships, and I'm able to articulate nearly everything with him, just short of where it concerns him. If I say I feel guilty, he can't hear that I don't mean about the person he dates openly who is currently in another city. I mean that I frustrate him every night. He thinks the impediment is elsewhere, guilt about this woman, that's why I can't have sex with him. I try to make clear that that is not it, and he doesn't trust me. It's like he tries to gather evidence against it: but you fucked me during the spring, but we've come so near it. I am making as clear as possible without explicitly insulting him that *I just don't want it*. I am not *swept*. I don't want to think during sex in the manner I might normally, especially if my thoughts are *I wish this were not happening*.

It's possible that if we were getting close again from a distance rather than from a shared apartment, my desire might be aroused in a different way. For instance. Of a particularly lovely conversation we shared yesterday over dinner, I thought, if we hadn't have been living together, I would have, after such a conversation, drafted him a sweet little email telling him how much it meant to me. The email would most likely make me anxious for a response, and the response would most likely be delayed or disappointing to me. As it is, if we're seeing each other in a couple of hours after other plans, there's no reason or chance to draft a little note, and there's no response to feel anxious for. No moment is that much more significant than any other.

How much of ambivalence is really just being terrified of another's departure or choice against you? How easily can you act the way you really want when you know you've both consented in some way to being *trapped*? I do feel trapped! Not explicitly by ruse, but in the sense of having fallen into something that wasn't at all what I anticipated, that I had good reason not to expect.

Apparently I told a new man at an art opening last night that "attachment is a violent form of love," and he wrote me saying he'd gotten home and jotted it down. It had me embarrassed, as though I'd stolen it from somewhere (I googled it; I hadn't).

Really, the most intimate thing to admit is your most shameful, irrational egotism: "I'm disappointed in almost everyone's thoughts but my own." I have admitted this to Max. Intimacy is many things.

"Where has your mind been this morning?" could be a very different sort of accusation than one might expect.

* * *

Living with Max is comforting but it makes me very sad. I think he's lovable, but I alternately, on occasion, find him lamentable or resentable. I'm judgmental with him like a mother, or perhaps more like a counsellor—an uninvested party—so he tells me everything. Maybe I don't *want* to know everything. Maybe it makes me frustrated with his character when he reveals not at all accidentally that he uses his Tinder app despite having, by all accounts, three loving girlfriends (Cybil, me, Lori, whom he chats with daily, spends lots of time with, and is clearly still attracted to). I admonish him: I can't begin to understand even what you think you want. He makes a comment that it's bizarre that I can be mad at him without really being mad. I tell him, plainly, I have no belief that he has any idea what he wants or what he is doing, so I am not invested in it. Sometimes it's the bluntest of what I say that he has no reaction to. Two nights ago we had penetrative sex, which I just wanted to go quickly, but he didn't bring himself to orgasm, and then I got frustrated and wanted it to stop, and he said, it looked like you were enjoying yourself, and I said, sure, I only stopped it once I'd really stopped enjoying myself but still prior to this I was playing it up because I thought you would come. There's no one but Max for whom my desire has been distributed this way: I want to be physically affectionate with him, but I never want to fuck him. He has a bit less physical affection toward me, but what he does have makes it so he'd like to fuck. Even our non-physical affection is so differently arranged. He's more likely to talk to me, invite me to something, want to be near if we're both a little happy, but *he's* unchanged: he's not exercising more, working more, or eating any differently than usual. I never really invite him to anything (since moving back in, I've mostly had one-on-one plans), I don't say as much to him, because when I'm stimulated, I come up with some abstraction, something I feel either makes more sense to write down for myself, or for Ivan or Maurice. I don't want to be next to him doing nothing while he chats on his phone. But I find that his presence moderates me and prevents me from eating badly or wasting time in certain compulsive ways. Even though I feel it is I who more explicitly rejects the idea that we have a primary relationship (on two accounts, which I don't euphemize with him: that his attention span bothers me and the sex isn't what I want), I still feel like I'm the one who loves him more. But It's not quantifiable like this.

Yesterday we went to the beach together with a group of his friends, and I didn't enjoy the trip. He was agitated on the way there and back and, I felt, aggressive toward me. Whereas when I experience needless worry (and I did, the time the landlord visited), I compensate by being twice as loving (he remarked upon this; I concurred). I think that when he was feeling grumpy, he badly needed to eat, and I have the luxury of having almost no stomach at all, so it never requires filling. Max must eat more than twice what I do, but still feels I'm not doing my share in the kitchen I don't use. There is no consumption issue that Max doesn't have, but my God, there is no one else to blame for this. Having him near can make me more eager to be attentive to that which he has little to do with. Life is fucking: a racket. I simultaneously wish I could go home to how it used to be—solitary—and fear totally that he, too, could come to consider it all too much and decide to leave. I do not want him to leave! I just don't want to have sex with him and pursuant to this do not want him as a romantic primary. Or: he *is* my romantic primary? Because he's who I come home to, and who I think about so much, and I have no interest in anyone else? But I don't want to fuck him, and later, when we don't live together, I don't want him to have the primacy anymore. I tell him, I have a good life: exercise, feel focused, not *too* focused, knock on wood, friends I love, one of them to come home to, masturbate successfully every morning and night, but he says he's so sad, and let's be honest, I'm sad, too! His friends at the beach were nice. You make a world together. You leave it. Miles and I have barely written since what we had to say to each other was, shit, you made my summer so good.

*　*　*

Seems clear: the one who feels more similar to and comprehensible to the other is the disadvantaged party. Even if you have no solitude or lonesomeness, you can find yourself anxious to spend time with whomever makes you feel most like *yourself.* To seek the presence of someone who fits you so well that you behave—with them and through them—as though they are not there. Are we better understood spending time with a diversity of people or are we better understood spending time with no one? I still love Max, but drunk I complain that we have nothing to talk about, or none of the same things to talk about, and how it's wonderful that nevertheless we've managed to make so much conversation. I love to cuddle with Max, to kiss his cheeks and neck. There's an angle from which he looks like the most handsome man there is. You think that if you separate yourself from a feeling of conjoinedness and mutual surveillance, you pry back from the world a life that is more authentically yours, but what truly happens is you're just miserable again. One articulates so well when miserable. There's such sharp thought in loneliness. Trouble is, it's so sharp it's scary, and it's pathetic when there's not even the promise of an audience. So people become artists. For the comfort of solitude with an audience.

Had an online chat with Ivan, who'd gotten a tattoo of some made-up symbol signifying his own artistry to himself. So he can take his shirt off and remember—*oh yes, I am an artist*. Is anyone in this dumb world even joking? Before this with Max and Lori and two others working in entertainment. Everyone was big and loud. I felt I couldn't be at my best, behaving this way. The lives of many: when I can't see them, they seem desirable to me, but once I'm with them, I understand why I had never been there before. I tell Max *everything*. I have no idea how it affects him. To what degree. Perhaps it doesn't. If you deliver information like it ought not provoke offence or hurt, this often works. Sadness is always worsened by another feeling it on your behalf, when you feel their shame. Behave as though nothing is wrong and it's easy to tell the man whose limp balls you sucked and kissed that afternoon, while he massaged his boner out, that you have no interest in and certainly nothing to contribute to his friends' conversations, though they're very lovely people. I was drunk last night lying down with Max, so I don't remember if, among other things, I told him I loved him, but if I said that, too, I'm sure I would have said it with little affect or emphasis. Ivan and I argued about the idea of living an authentic or inauthentic life. I couldn't tolerate what he meant. Everyone's life is an authentic realization of their desires and values drawn out through choices that invite consequences, which further inform what they want, within certain constraints. He says at the end of it that if you have regrets, you haven't lived authentically. I think, no, dissatisfaction is not the same thing: that's simply *having regrets*. We all get what we want. I want to be poor and alone with a diversity of confidences and affections, reading a lot. I guess. It's exciting and invigorating to feel like you must win people over, because, although terrifying, it means you're being challenged, and you can imagine a better world welcoming you. But feeling as though there's no one to impress has its benefits, too, in stability and sanity. One always longs to feel the opposite way. I feel good.

Yesterday afternoon with Max, after he came, he said, still glazed over, he wants to see me masturbate, wants to see me make myself come. I said back to him without even thinking, "I'll take that under consideration."

* * *

It is autumn and I am filled with love. I can't escape what I have no option but to return home to. If speakability is love's essence, oh God. Things are so fucking sayable. Things are sayable absolutely without impediment. No impediment; speakability; filled with love.

Days lately have been very dense. I never know when anything happens.

Each party gets the gift of vulnerability of the other. It's like all today is my orgasm.

* * *

It is very bad to have a very bad husband, and tiresome to recount, even if the density of living with someone means all the misbehaviour is so *detailed*. Here's what Rancière has to say about attention, back in *The Ignorant Schoolmaster*—I can't find it. My husband is tricking me. This is what's worst about my husband. My husband just wants to feel powerful as he's wanted for years because of his attention problems, among other things.

Normally when I step out of my husband, I'm fine, but he lives here, so I don't get many opportunities. I don't need anything from my husband. I don't need love from him, and I don't need devotion, and I don't need care. I prefer to be the one who gives affection. And my husband prefers to receive it. That's why we're here. Or he prefers his girlfriend elsewhere who perhaps loves him a different way. What was the Rancière quote about attention? Oh, who knows. That attention is not an ability—it's a *decision*, and if you don't make a decision to grant it to anyone, it reveals contempt both of them and of yourself. I *vocalize* not wanting him but also my love for him. Last night was the best night we'd had together, and then tonight he had a phone call with Cybil? Like when Lori was here in the apartment this week. I can't do enough for him. I *won't*. Threat of loss stuns me into beginning to ask for things I *know* that I have *said* that I do not want from my *fucking husband*. How and why should the less desiring party be so much more devoted.

* * *

Everyone bothers me except my husband who bothers me. This is how one sits in place in the world.

I'll never have the time to recount all of what is said in my conversations with Max, and plenty of it is very funny. I feel as though he puts me into competition with others unnecessarily, to test me. Told him, of having Lori over, in the bath, "What you are doing, I am not doing." One moment I'll speak with clarity and confidence, articulating myself exactly, and the next moment he turns some new corner, stunning me again. I feel scared and desperate. Despite this, I can't promise him my *future*. I can promise him my present. I can promise him that I'll never put people into competition with him. I can promise him that even if the sex isn't what I want, I'm satisfied. We'll have what felt at the time to me like the most emotionally frank conversation we've had, or that I've perhaps had with anyone, in and after the bath, and then the next night he'll ask if I'm comfortable returning to a platonic relationship again, and for a few hours I'll feel like I've been struck across the head. But say one part of said bath conversation was him asking, finally, "What do *you* want from *me*?" and me having no answer for him. Say this morning over coffee—we had sex last night; I felt desperate—he says, "You don't want to be with me," and I say, "I *do* want to be with you *now*." On other occasions, it's more like he's rejecting me, but for what, I am she who gives him comfort! I've seen other people lately. Dinner with Freida and then a visit to a gallery opening, where I did lots of fun chatting the night that preceded the bath. Working at the library. Exercising on the days I don't feel nausea. Why am I willing to give up more in service of something that I want less? School starts tomorrow. Linguistics classes first. Max says he knows when I'm aggravated with him, because it's on those occasions that I'll make hurtful comments about his character. He doesn't, ever, about mine. But I'm on much better behaviour. Over email, told Noah—who's coming next weekend to defend his PhD— that he couldn't stay here anymore due to an unanticipated advancement in a life that moves very quickly. He said, "I hope you mean quickly someplace good." I said, "Noah, maybe I've stopped trying to make judgments on the quality of my life!" I'm not miserable. I feel stress, often, but it vacillates with comfort, and the comfort comes with little effort on my part. *Time fucking is dense.* If I had more of it to myself I'd gain the perspective necessary to understand *what is really going on.* What is happening is what's going on. Do I want to *decode desires*? Do I want to reveal some truth of how our actions demonstrate an enduring teleological desire? Little would bear this out. We are both acting in service of what we desire during the moments we are together. To touch and to comfort. Ever as I grow, I'm still made to kiss the neck of a complaining man with a handsome face. I keep changing and so do my values, but this continues to satisfy something very primal in me. At the gallery, I spoke to a playwright who said, of comics and actors: they are incredibly brave, and incredibly desperate. And they bring it out in others. I don't mind suffering uncertainty when the object of my affection doesn't make me feel like I'm missing something or can't qualify. Ninety per cent of what's happening I'm not even *doing*. This is his complicated life, and I just live here. *Two fucking weeks.* Each day I am high on pot, but yesterday he came home high on coke, and I was regretful that he hadn't invited me to that party. Funny that Max and I shouldn't know what we want from each other when it's actually so clear: someplace for our words to go, each night. What else. That we'll keep too watchful an eye on each other for either of us to get depressed when autumn comes. Maybe I *will* stop making judgments on the quality of my life. Maybe the details of feeling aren't the truth of feeling—the truth is the action you commit to.

* * *

I'll always be fucking to standard. That's a gift God doesn't offer us all. Domesticity satisfies me and will presumably continue to satisfy me until I suspect it of depriving me of other things. I have a good life and I watched a good movie with Blaise last night, but I was dozing off because of all the talking with Max the night prior, and then with Blaise I was not a valuable conversation partner. I came home and slept alone, early, solid, and this morning ironed Max's outfit for Rosh Hashanah as he prepared for me a coffee and a bowl of fruit, or he prepared the bowl of fruit for himself and didn't have time to eat it. He said. Recounting the domestic is funny because you'd recount none of it were you alone. It is not notable; it is the consistent texture of life. I ironed his shirt imperfectly. My wife, she's terrible. I prefer our life with no obstacles, honestly.

First classes feel good and sharp and brought memories of a feeling of divine sadness for Marianne, who has too much wit and attention and creativity for this world—I thought, she sought her faith because God gave her too much, and in *spending* her gifts, she could never be repaid sufficiently by others. But what does God give those who produce too much? God sometimes gives them generous departmental funding, at Oxford, where she started her PhD this fall.

What if love, which I had assumed would be a corrective, really acts more as a kind of anti-inflammatory?

What if the only stressful thing is thinking that your desire must be wise and responsible, that it must account for the desire of all parties? If your desire is humble, and knows it knows only itself, it is secure. And if you don't even bother to desire and skip straight to enjoyment: nothing, *nothing* beats this.

No proper relationships mean that no one *serves a function* for you. They are just themselves. They are more complicated than they're worth. And yet we choose them.

Trust is bizarre and takes too many forms to speak of. Like, I trust that I know what to expect of you. I trust that you won't subject me to more than I am prepared for. I trust that I know you, and I know how you're bound to behave. With some you only experience a trust that is solipsistic. Or, until the day you stop, your orgasms are still your own to give.

I pray that people retain their inability so that I may continue to find them *adorable*, which isn't very kind at all.

* * *

It occurs to me that you can moderate an appetite without satisfying it, but it doesn't occur to everyone. You can suppress. Wilfully or by circumstance. But should you?

It's bizarre that someone might have the ability to soothe you against the very discomfort they have caused you. I always avoid knowing this. It's what families are built upon. There are those who cause discomfort by pushing and those who cause discomfort by pulling, and I suppose I know which of these I live with. How many times have I told Max that our relationship is familial though we handle each other's genitals probably daily. I don't want to lose what I love to another. I mean my interests. My heart palpitations are back, but Max still suffers worse, on a daily basis, from feelings of purposelessness and lack of direction. He speaks of my lust like it's a decision and this doesn't sound *wrong*. You forget when you live a certain way that maybe you could have another version of the same thing, which would be better suited to you. Honestly, you both could. He said I was a universe. Who isn't. In whose world is it not a different world.

It's not that I think I don't deserve pleasure, just that I don't think anyone else should have to give it to me. At least no one I've known yet. It's so hard to tell someone, in order for me to come, you'd have to leave the room.

* * *

Catherine Millet line about intestines working according to primitive software popped into my head, because *me too*: I work according to primitive software. I got drunk and blacked out and threw up and put up further divisions between me and my love. In order to prove my shame to myself? What if you then come home and your sweetheart is still there, even if you aren't sure of him? I found it impossible to recount for Caroline the last *two and a half weeks* in all their density, and then when we went to a concert together, I felt fucking *high*. Many strangers, young people, new people, beautiful people, people I wanted to meet, bands playing music that sounded like the 1990s that I was nostalgic for musically because my lover taught me about those times in the mid-2000s. The diversion I enacted was I fucked some very handsome stranger boy simply because I could, I guess, or I wanted to feel again what it would be like to fuck a young, healthy, virile person. And what is it like? It's like anything else: exercise, and it's better coming home to the man whose face you hold even if you feel you've been tricked into the relationship. I felt ashamed today and slept through all my classes, in the park and in the chapel at Hart House, because Max, whom I'd cheated, was at home. Hungover and sad, felt doomed to myself. It was sweet when I got home. Shame and guilt compress when we're alone, but present with others, you just go on. It makes sense that people do any number of terrible things to others simply learning that what you don't bring up or think about almost hasn't happened. Last night's blackout was my first in months, but it doesn't mean entering a new phase of blackouts; it was *a night*. There have been days when I've felt good and secure and like Max is a centring force and makes me whole. There have been days when I've felt focused and disciplined. There have also been days like today, which I brought upon myself.

* * *

Even shared, my life can be purified. I asked last night if Max still planned to go back to another and he said, "No," and I said, "*Good*." I haven't told him what I did. I feel horrible for my compulsions. I feel horrible for having my cunt scraped out within minutes of throwing up uncontrollably by someone whose last name I don't know, whose health I don't know. I don't trust Max so I want to construct an equivalence with my own behaviour. I *wanted to*. I'm done.

* * *

I'm going to reach the point where I can no longer articulate what I feel, because it barely matters, because the conclusions I can draw from feeling don't much contribute to my decision-making. I love Max, but he is tiresome, and was very hurt when I told him that sometimes I couldn't tell whether he only had a mood disorder or if he really sometimes couldn't access the reality that others access. To be hurt by this, he took a break from being hurt by Cybil, who is sending him very unkind text messages about their breakup, and was that my intention? How much he complains about Cybil to me is the primary reason I think his mind is unable to comprehend that which lies outside it. I told him, it seems to me you misbehave with people in order that they may demonstrate excessive care for you. He resisted this and anyway spoke of suicide. Saw Freida yesterday, in the morning. She says, Catherine, don't be a sex mommy to this old man. She says, imagine being a real mommy to a grateful new being that you give the world to? What you have is no substitute. And so, I say, *yes, but we speak so openly!* With a baby, it would take years before an emotionally frank conversation. In the afternoon I saw Ruby enact a Hasidic ritual in North York wherein she swung a hen by its wings around her shoulders, transferring her sins to it, so it could be shipped to Montreal, sacrificed, and fed to the poor. I thought, that's so funny, before your sins are absolved, they sit cooped up with all the sins of everyone else for six hours on their way to Montreal. Nothing is instant. I'm not going to tell Max about my sin because his hold on reality suffers as it is. Regarding Max, only Ruby has given me the advice that seems right: it's neither terribly good nor terribly bad, but it does seem like it's happening. On Friday night I cried lots with my mother over dinner when she said she couldn't remember a time in life when she was happy, and I inferred from this that I've never made her happy. I told Max. And then him with the suicide stuff, and then me, like, do you understand how horrible it is for me to hear that—I'm with you *every day*. If you're a salve, you'd like at least to be effective. I want to build a home with Max as though it were forever even though: *absolutely not*. I have a very disciplined intellect I must inspire so that I may have the life I want. The life I want now, with Max, isn't the life I want later, without him. There are models for fidelity to the present alone. It's equally that I will never fill this man up and that I do not want to. You don't have to make others prove an excess of love. I tell him: *Just slow down*. Who am I talking to? I used to recount my life in paragraphs but I don't get the luxury of experiencing it like this anymore. Instead other luxuries, like a kiss to each breast, each morning.

Annual checkup. On first look, even cervical, there seems to be nothing wrong with me. Told young, cute resident physician that I was experiencing chest pains again like earlier in the summer, but that, again, I was stressed. Explained to him my living situation in a brief synopsis. He goes to consult with my primary doctor about whether or not I should be put on anxiolytics. He thinks, probably not, if things don't become dire. Returns, asks, "But in your living situation, you're safe?" I say, "Oh! Yes, of course. I'm aggravated, but I'm safe." He calls me "twenty-five years young," and I remark that he doesn't look much older, and look where he is in *his* life! He says that I am right, but that's neither here nor there, and it doesn't relate to whether or not I'm suffering from a heart condition. He's not exactly correct about this.

* * *

It's difficult to accept—or not to be menaced by—the prospect that you can be whatever you'd like, even with someone else in the room. Someone can know all ostensibly knowable things about you (family life, dating history, eating habits, writing style, *grooming habits*) and still not inhibit or constrain you. You accept them, too, imperfect, because it makes the most sense to. It is the choice that brings the most pleasure and comfort to you both. I don't get all the sleep I want. Otherwise, mostly, life is better. It's a kind of magic: being handled gently and lovingly on a daily basis makes the world less menacing, because *you*—your person, your body, your being—*have a home*. It feels good right now. In the middle of the night kissing sleepily, he asks, "Are we in love?" and I answer, "We are."

* * *

Even if it were true that a love that does more than serve a function is simply a love wherein you confuse yourself with the beloved, I still need more sleep at night for better concentration during the day. Love is good. Tonight no plans, but I sure hope Max has some. Got a sty this morning. There is a man I woke with who is witness to each of my ailments and gave me crazy head last night during our little Leonard Cohen listening party. Really fucking great. That I can't come is a travesty. What is to be done? You suspect conversation will be finite, but it never is, particularly if your husband recounts his meals for you with the brilliantly illustrative awe of a toddler. It will be weird later in when I have privacy but I don't have love. I'll always have love. Fidelity to the events.

* * *

Contemplation takes solitude; spedness takes contemplation; infatuation takes spedness (in my experience). I have no solitude in my apartment, which is also my lover's.

Desire in solitude can facilitate *extreme cognitive activity*. Your understanding of philosophy, the world, and your lover circuit together continually. Each seeks an explanation in the other. So you devise *many* because you're driven to do so, imagining you can recover some explanation that reveals the correct path toward getting what you want (or, otherwise, toward cleansing yourself of the need to want it). But when both parties say yes? When they say yes, and further spend all their time together? I am completely in love, but it seeks no explanation. I seek no pathway out of it, nor any way to burrow further in. I feel happy. I wouldn't mind, however, intense cognitive aptitude. I just want none of the insecurity I'm sure would come with it.

It's possible that the only things partners need to share are sincerity, a definition of fidelity, and a similar respective propensity for guilt and shame. Discussing fidelity, I told Max: it's so easy to imagine sleeping with only one person, but so difficult—and completely undesirable—to imagine sharing with only one person the best and most intimate conversations. He agrees.

It's been nicer since we've avowed ourselves to each other. Our conversations have taken a kinder, more focused tone. Avowals of love have been daily—often Max wakes to make them in the middle of the night. Our sleep quality together hasn't been half-bad, though semi-conscious make-outs have been interspersed through each night.

Right now things are fucked-idyllic and neither of us seems to understand how this could possibly be. I love him. I love *it*. What I have with Max I've really never had with anyone, and I get the impression that this is also so for him, although he has already cohabited. *Sayability.* I feel like it's impossible that couples ever understand each other like Max and I do, that they ever have our honesty and patience. The jokes. It's difficult for someone to annoy you when everything they say is in this self-correcting and modulating torrent of discovery, bouncing off you. We both worry about work. This morning, he says, "I wish I could monetize your affection." I say, "You could! You'd just have to outsource it."

* * *

Two nights ago, Max said sleepily (we had been out earlier, drinking, at shows), "I wish I could drag you everywhere." The visual it produced in my mind was that I was unconscious, bleeding, led by a leash. It wasn't some sex thing. He did not even have a boner saying it. Is love what one feels for another when they behold them and think, I could drag that rag doll with me by a rope? But then we have conversations the following day, and I feel love is less strictly that feeling. It is that feeling together with others. It's the tension of wanting a privileged being to be both entirely containable and entirely excessive, and to navigate in the space of this tension. In love, the other is simultaneously something growing, expanding, unknowable, and *all mine*.

My linguistics textbook warns, "Remember, domination is a containment relation." I do still read what the world doesn't intend into my love, fine.

I notice my days are better, and my concentration, too, when we've slept in separate beds, and he hasn't told me he's had thoughts of suicide. You have to ensure yourself some good days!

* * *

It's good, I guess, that I'm sensitive to dominant behaviour, because what this keen eye allows me to see is that it's not really happening. As we fall into our rhythm, I see that Max's particular style of codependence, as moderated for my own tendencies, doesn't suit me so badly. I almost wasn't ready for how good Max would be at this relationship once we decided to call it one. I feel loved; I love him. I feel turned on; he does, too. He invites me out for a night with him and his friends; I invite him out for drinks after I see a movie with Blaise. This is just the recountable stuff. Being with Max changes the way I feel as a person in the world; it is changing my attachment to solitude as a baseline of being. He is making being with another my new default for relaxation. He is making it so being with him is the most natural way I know to be myself. He, or my commitment to him, has finally made it so I've masturbated to orgasm with no moments of external videographic aid. For the first time! And the next day, a second. I have finally been able to bring myself to orgasm only with fantasies I conjure myself. Still, the first time, the fantasy was a bit external: I was watching Max fuck slash eat Cybil out. After a few minutes, I came to my mind's projection of him eating her ass out while looking at me shamefully like, I'm sorry, just a minute, I can't help it. It felt appropriate that weaning myself off pornography, I might first imagine pleasure at the site of other bodies. It is not bizarre that the only visual fantasies I can conceive of are triangulated.

* * *

Pause: if a panic attack is anything, it's just: total psychological and somatic concordance (10x speed) and asking the god who finally knows you and is known to you, please, don't let anyone steal my things while I lie down on the sidewalk in a near-comatose state of absence for the next twenty minutes.

* * *

I wish I could have both my love and my solitude, but it hasn't turned out this way. As I wrote, I had a panic attack last night, and I haven't come back to life since. Walking home during the evening from a lecture, I felt sunny, and then speedy, and then like I could string discrete things together into the linguistic structures I'd just learned, and suddenly some unrelated thoughts came together in a way that felt inarticulably just right, and then I felt some light nausea and a tingle of warmth throughout my body that together with some fast and frankly weird thoughts made me feel like I was high on mushrooms, and then I realized how hot and sweaty I suddenly was, and how quickly my heart was beating, so I took my coat off, folded it up, and placed my head upon it as I lay on my back, eyes closed, on the foot of someone's lawn. Careful not to have anything stolen, knowing I should allow myself to slide into any state of (un)consciousness I needed, I slid my arm through the loops of my knapsack. And lay there panting for about twenty minutes, though it felt like no time at all. Then I was hungry. I was able to curb the heart palpitations quickly, so they didn't make me scared. Prior to the attack, it had been an average day. I know that, for a period of time, the way I was contemplating my lecture on my walk felt like a feat of retention. I don't know when I started to feel like syntactic theory was suddenly collecting too much. I felt happy about Max, and he had texted me during lecture to say that he was at his parents' house and wanted to tell them about me, but it was complicated. He said he showed his mother my picture, called me his roommate, and she said I looked nice.

Another detail about Max: the night after the rag-doll dragging comment, he said that his American work visa, which he'd initiated the process for almost two years ago, was finally approved. I had plans with Caroline and didn't want to talk about it. My fear, then, was that he'd leave immediately, which I did not want to hear. When I got home, we talked about it, and that wasn't his plan. It is roughly the same as it had been short-term: stay here during the fall and over Christmas, try to schedule as much work as possible to go to New York in January. And this is what I'd wanted, anyway. Living with Max is lovely but also hard for me in ways that a sense of guilt and propriety don't allow me to make known. I wish I had the luxury he has, that sometimes I were at home alone all morning and afternoon while he saw to a responsibility outside the house. It's hard. It's hard when I don't feel well. On the one hand, he attends to me expertly, and physical touch brings me back to the world. On the other hand, if I feel miserable and antsy, I'd just like to feel that way for whatever amount of time I must, and not share myself with him or feel the pressure to be present. I want to go to bed early and sleep in obscenely. I don't want to talk. I want to write every awful thing that occurs to me and not share some lighter version of it as dialogue. I don't want to be made to feel better. I don't want to share in love. I don't want to talk about the two of us moving together because it's no good here when I'm still not near graduation and I won't have anything to do there and I'll have to make all my friends from scratch and I won't have a job. I don't want to go anywhere with this man unless I learn that he has some fucking discipline, because if he has nothing to do and I have nothing to do and all we do then is give each other an excuse to stream video content on the internet while fondling each other, I will wish to God that I had another fucking life wherein I gave anything to the world!

* * *

Max and I agree that the love we have for each other doesn't destabilize our lives with worry, which is good, but it can steal us from our responsibilities if all we do is cuddle and talk, which is as good a kind of bad as I've ever known. I cried in front of Caroline, recounting my panic attack and how little I want to be cared for when I don't even know what's wrong with me, how much I was used to mental health matters being private, how nervous it made me to extend responsibility for my health to anyone else. I think I said, "I don't want anyone to look after me! I just want to look after myself!" and teared up, embarrassed at the most legible parental issues possible. Then I came home to Max, whom some part of each day I

183

don't want, but who then fills me with such joy. My mind is doing the work of transforming the body of the woman I masturbate to into one that might be mine. My mind is doing the work to put me in the pleasure room while I am being hit. Max has this joke about an alcoholic failing to remember beating up his brother's father, and what's the term for one's brother's father? It's cute. I'm always in the room for pleasure living with him.

Caroline assures me the beginning is always like this, where you take up such obscene portions of the other's time. But it isn't always. Then you get back to work.

* * *

Yesterday I had a selection of feelings and thoughts that had nothing whatsoever to do with Max, which felt very healthy. School social. There weren't many free drinks. Morgan was there and lovely to talk to. He's quit drinking because he sees himself as having no control over his life, and worse still he might be correct. He has trouble with everything, but speaks, writes, and thinks in such flexible and inventive ways. I tell him, I wish you worked better, and I wish everyone with a sensibility like either of ours worked better, so that we produced the culturally dominant things. He laughed and said this sounded nice.

Left social early to see Max perform two shows. Friends of his I'd seen lately. One of them I get along with enormously well. She'd heard lots about me and was stunned excited. So fun; talked so fast; I felt as though I was being forcefully initiated as a member of Comedy Couples. Frightening but safe. There were glows. I said, we are not a Comedy Couple: I work in a library, and I would like in the future to teach. No one should be unhappy to find themselves trapped by kindness. The walk home, though rainy, was delightful, because it was clear to Max that I'd had a terrific time. Then another gigantic, affectionate bedtime conversation like the others. Max's constant vocalization of his will to carry this relationship out for the rest of our lives sometimes makes me fear he's in some sort of exceptional mental state that will later seem like a dream. Like, when he stops thinking this, he won't need time to adjust and recover and detach himself from the idea of spending our lives together, he'll just wake up one day and think, what the fuck was that?

We almost always sleep together now. At night, he always asks, and I almost always say yes. He begged yesterday in the kitchen as we first arrived home, "Please, don't leave me too soon." I said I had no plans to. It's the sheer extent of his displayed vulnerability that makes me think it's not unlikely that he's a victim of self-hypnosis and he's bound to snap out of it, but how could one snap when there's no fucking resistance? Affection's not physical! But Lord, does it ever have such a number of physical expressions. We always kiss just right. I remember at the beginning of September that he wasn't kissing in a way that felt good to me, but of course, how could he have been, when I hadn't been there to kiss? Then you adapt to what the other wants and settle together on a tradition of touch that's only yours together. And it's just fucking right! And you even do it in public a bit. A bit. Nothing crazy. But you're a Comedy Couple now and your friends think there's really some potential there, so what's to be hidden? You think there's another person for you, better suited to you, but there isn't. All there are are millions and millions of other whomeverthefuck people and then someone who has committed himself to how to be himself for you. Together you come upon a form. A tradition. A relationship! And nothing else could beat it, because nothing else has learned how.

Honestly, I'd never known it was possible to be so consumed while being so unafraid and unselfconscious. Until now, I'd only thought consumption was fear and self-consciousness. I suppose this is what people are talking about (when they are talking about [love]).

* * *

My life has been reduced to a pleasant simplicity visible in (a portion of) my last email to Ivan, here:

> Time is nice. I had four Thanksgiving meals to go to and I feel like one of life's luckiest women. Nothing is difficult. Domestic living is better than I would ever expect, though I do eat more sharing space with a man with a bigger appetite. I talk more sharing space with a man with a bigger appetite for conversation. I am amenable to these things. This morning he told me apropos ?? that people who take black coffee are statistically more likely to be psychopaths (I take my coffee black). Max! Life's great.

But otherwise in my notes for school I write, "PRIVACY IS THE ONLY DEPRIVATION THAT GIVES," waiting for dawdling Max to leave the fucking house so I can get a fucking _hour_ to do anything by myself.

It matters less what you want than what you have, especially in the case that what you have is quite good and will spend the winter in the USA.

186

I've stopped watching pornography. Weaning was a process. Part of it Max, thinking of his facial expressions and dick and sweetness. Part of it is my commitment *to* Max, the intent on forming a sexuality for myself that doesn't always seek to latch on to some external image. But primarily, I think, it was giving myself to fantasies of something that looks so stupid and obscene as the porn I would otherwise be watching.

* * *

I feel like every day since fucking I've written myself some variant of "Not a dick is a lithium pill!" But I cannot escape the truth of this world. I love Max's warm and stabilizing body, and I stay calm attached to it for hours I might in the past have thought to designate to other things. Twenty minutes alone allowing my mind to wander wherever it wills itself to, I get so *hyper*. It is like: reading faster, music playing louder, more attention to both, some dancing or exercise, *running through the apartment*. Too much energy to do anything. Then otherwise none, no energy at all. Only with another I care for is my energy in any way focused. Slowed yet not to a stop. Max at this very moment is at the doctor for more Dexedrine and I *should* be on my way to class; he was late, too!

Silently I cracked myself up this morning, and Max asked, "What?" And I said, "I don't know: It's the end! It's over! I don't want anything but to be touching you, and that's one form of death!"

Funny when once, "Why does he want all the world's attention? Why isn't mine enough?" When now, "Why does he want *my* attention? Why isn't all the world's enough!?"

Before I left, I masturbated to pornography for the first time since the day I vowed not to, realizing that last night with Max, during the mutual masturbation, even to maintain control over my erotic imaginary isn't to bring it together with the erotic real, which might still be a hurdle. And this afternoon, I didn't want orgasm to be an exercise in the examination of my psyche. I just wanted some external virtual presentation. Too many hours with Max, and the investigation of what he is for me erotically can make me sad. I want to remind myself of all those other stupid shiny things there outside myself.

I CANNOT DO THIS, AND I KNOW I CANNOT DO THIS, AND I have known that I cannot do this since it began. My relationship with Max does not suit me and I wouldn't have chosen it. I never *did* choose it. I just had foisted upon me something I have been rejecting consistently for three years. Parts of it feel nice, yes. How couldn't they? Cuddling and laughing are for all purposes very nice. But there is nothing of Max's that doesn't infringe upon me. I have tried to convince myself, you can adapt! You can learn what a relationship is and put limits before it! This is only the beginning; beginnings are always rocky!

But *why?* Why must setting aside time for myself be done in such a way so as not to hurt the feelings of someone I have no duty to? Why am I woken at 6:00 a.m., before work, to console a man who feels he's at the end of his life who just fucking *moved into my house?* Max is in a tremendously difficult period in his life: his father is dying, and he is not getting paid work. I can't do anything about either of these things but console him, which I do *every day*, and it takes me from my own responsibilities, which are important. Which, if I do not honour, will make it so I go through a very difficult period in my life. Max cannot cope. I cannot help him through the shame he feels considering wage work because he has too little to occupy himself and too little money coming in. I do not know how to offer support with upcoming familial loss when I have only the most detached relationship to my own family. I don't know. The luckiest person's parents shall die. Unless your own life is particularly unfortunate, it's a guarantee. I just feel like so much of what I say to him is wasted labour. It effects no change, yet it is still my duty. But if we were not in a relationship, it would not be my duty. And if he didn't live in my fucking house, we would not be in a relationship.

I do not talk through my problems with Max. Nor, significantly, with anyone—certainly not to the extent that he does. He nevertheless offers up "solutions" for things I haven't volunteered as problems. I just want us to be two focused, self-sufficient people who do not worsen the day of the other. But instead all we are are bad parents to each other.

On coming home to Max: I don't usually look forward to it. On days that I'm drained, I know I can't go home to rest, so I just stay ambling around on campus not working, not resting, unhappy, doing nothing much. I'm more eager to return home on the chance that he is elsewhere.

I, too, am wasting his time. He thinks I give him something, but I don't.

I feel scared that setting boundaries will cause him to be upset with himself, and feel more depressed than he already would be, and speak further about suicide, and be inactive and maybe destructive in ways I haven't even seen. I fear that saying I don't want to be with him long-term will invite a very hostile living situation, where he is even more depressive than he is now.

I don't want to be callous. Things are not easy for him. But he is not being kind. He is not tempering his experience in order to be kind. He knows, after years, what gets me going. He has come to know that his need of care will inspire more from me than a will to offer it. He's adorable. And he often behaves with kindness and gentleness toward me. And he plays himself off as such a guileless, incompetent little doofus that who in the world could think he was manipulative?! But Max is *not stupid*, and he knows. He knows that when he tells me—my day has been so bad, will you forgive me? I smoked. I'm terrible. I shouldn't be allowed to live—that I will say, oh, my sweetheart, lie down with me: you'll always have me! He knows that I will put down whatever I'm doing to say it, too.

It's not crazy that I might be manipulated with tactics I mostly recognize from my family—it only makes fucking sense! It makes sense that they are common tactics for familial/conjugal dominance and that I, specifically, am attracted to them. I know this. Why is it that, since rejecting Max, I've still been attracted to him? There is something primal in the crush I got on him as a performer fucking *ten years ago* that isn't easy to cast away fully, because it has to do with childhood attachment. It's almost mystical how well Max brings together my relationship with *both* of my parents, and how perfectly, by chance, he's managed to capitalize on my feelings of duty. To what? We've been dating for *a fucking month*, and we speak as though we're married!

Nothing is right and I will not forgive myself if I let this fuck up another semester of school. Not now. Another sign that dominance has succeeded: when you credit your dominator with the relative calm and security you feel. *It's not Max.* I had an emotionally and philosophically rich summer where I read, studied, socialized, and calmed down. I came home feeling prepared for the year. That I've avoided the school anxieties I felt last year isn't because of Max—it's me. And if I'm doing anything for Max, I have to stop it. I don't want to. It's not my responsibility. It's taking away my responsibility to my own life.

It's no surprise that I can be loved, and less still that it would happen when I feel a responsibility to be at a sad man's service. I do not need what this love gives me.

And what is that? What does it give?

Like it gives him: daily touch and a feeling of support in life's cracks. I get sad. I get sad because I do not have traditionally stable family support and I often place a great deal of importance on the affection and praise of less-than-reliable people. Max in my life makes me think less of who isn't calling me and what emails I'm not receiving. He makes me think less of how little speaking or writing I'm either doing or being asked to do.

This doesn't mean I need Max. It means I should invest less in unreliable friends and cherish my reliable ones better. It means I should not economize so much when it comes to contact, period. I should, in fact, care just as much about writing and speaking as I do when I'm without him, and I shouldn't feel ashamed when I have school to do, too. I should ask people to spend time with me. I should go out and socialize. I should just invest as little as I do when I'm with Max in who should call me first (when I'm with Max, *everyone* calls me first).

A relationship is a way to be affirmed. To the outside world. "Congratulations." Someone has said yes to you. And you to them. You've made a commitment. You are adults. In the case of Max and me, it seems our commitment to each other ensures that we are *not* adults.

There is this sort of curiosity: wanting to know what you'll be like with a person, under them, as though having come out the other side of something. But it seems I may already know.

* * *

Poor Max and I just want our best lives, from which we aren't as far as we think. I'm so prepared to minimize my life and blame him for having done so, but I'm less prepared to confront, legitimately, how momentous this is. Max is a sweetheart and I am ungrateful.

Max is good to me, and he is good, having trouble. He's not having trouble to trick me. His fucking dad is not fucking dying in order that I may be trapped! Max's kindness and generosity are just things I barely have any context for. And *the way we talk*. Nothing is forbidden. Most is a joke. A utopia you don't need to be excused from for your low moods. I'd always thought it was a dream. I've never in my life made with anyone what I've made with Max, and indeed, *I have made it, too*. How could it be that someone gives me so much without threatening me with anything more than the fact that it may continue?

Murder-suicide is primarily recast as fodder for jokes, too, which is better. All the shit folded into our love. Some as masturbation fantasies, others as jokes. (I don't remember if I've written yet, as Max and I discussed what makes our relationship work, he suggested that most people would prefer to cut their limbs off than to share the better part of the conversations we love so much.) I suppose he understands better what people enjoy, and that is why he is a comic. Because with all our talk of death and sickness and perversion and inadequacy, all I think is that everyone must wish they had a relationship like ours!

* * *

No more computer orgasm. No more demolishing consciousness and funnelling in some substitute. If I'm not feeling desirous enough to bring myself to orgasm, perhaps I shouldn't be having one. An orgasm I give myself is a new practice of commitment and focus. Of *meditation*, insofar as I have to direct myself, without losing the thread, to a very pure form of thought. That's why, on the best mornings we've had, Max and I wake up early—he goes one room over to meditate his way while I stay in bed and do mine, and then breakfast. This makes me feel good. He likes to make a big, slow breakfast and listen to a podcast, and at this time I usually prefer to return to my bedroom with a coffee to read something. Attention to his ritual can also be attention to my own, too. All is fine and will be fine. Nobody wants to end my life. Nobody even wants to take it.

* * *

I love Max, certainly, but I'm not sure his love for me has much effect. I worked all summer for this kind of freedom but I'm not sure it's in the interest of what I'm trying to undertake at present. Last night, friends together for drinks. It was lovely. Oswald, Blaise, Morgan, Marianne. Mentioned Max and new demands of beholdenness. I feel a great deal of warmth toward Oswald, which was not something I expected to see in my future when I selected him from the mist for haphazard casual sex under a rain curtain of mania some night back in April. I talked so much about my worry that if I didn't somehow find the right path for it soon, I'd never be able to form a career from what I hope are my intellectual talents. He said he's not worried: he'll find something from which he can earn wages, and write just as he'd like without the worry of gaining popularity. I envy or admire this. I think it's how I felt when I was younger, before I understood that people *could* capitalize on their creative pursuits to earn a living so they didn't have to have some other, separate thing. Oswald's comfort with this doesn't come from a place of naïveté. He knows about careerism. It just doesn't concern him. He brought me a copy of a collection of poetry he just compiled from his friends for release at a bar. (No price, just the polite request that you buy a drink for a contributor.) I was not there the night he released it. I was at home, probably cuddling with Max.

* * *

When solitude is all you've known, it forms your basis for life. You consider it your resting state. Doesn't mean it's better.

Spend less time interrogating your ambivalence. You've made your choice. It's rather a beautiful one. If you don't want your life restricted, don't restrict yourself. It's not him: it's you.

* * *

I fear I'll give something up to Max, offer him care that I don't require the equivalent of, and then when he's done grieving, he'll be done with me, too. I have some experience with this. Max is not a parent of mine. He has such concerted, devoted focus upon me. What I've learned can happen is not happening. He's good to me, and he needs care, because a profoundly difficult thing is happening in his life.

He has now joined me in joking, almost serious: no one has what we have.

*　*　*

One wants someone with whom to perform the thing after having lived a mostly normative life. Another has a fair bit of trouble explaining her mostly non-normative life to him, and the way it makes it so that each one of her experiences is different from his. Not curable, different.

Max's father passed away on the day of my last entry. Max had been spending his nights at the hospital for a few days, expecting it. He texted me about it while I was eating with my mother, who I saw for the first time since she got home from Morocco, where she was married to her internet boyfriend, Yasin. We met in a coffee shop instead of the usual lobby of her workplace, which I took to indicate something unfortunate, and I was correct. She had been let go earlier that week, just after coming back from Morocco, and had been told that she could go home immediately. The dinner, however, was good. Talked a lot about Max. Even though my mother seems to have just thrown herself into a new yoke of dominance, she's very attentive to fears that I might be doing so as well. She has recently seen a new therapist, one she likes. She recounted to me, mystified, that he finally made her see that she needed some purpose regarding work, labour, her own abilities. This is unreal. Good for her for finding the stranger finally equipped to guide her to this realization. During too much talk about history and family and guidance and relationships, I understood that despite all she wouldn't give me as a child, despite all the comfort and care and security I lacked, she could at least deliver me toward something that was never hers until it was too late: freedom and independence, and the will to claim some individual purpose at as early an age as possible.

Came home that evening to be ready to receive Max, worried for his state, but oddly, it seemed improved from earlier in the week. It finally happened. So much of the stress Max experienced was due to seeing his father in pain, confused, unable to do anything—to be witness to this weakness. This night was sweet. It was easy to be there for him. He was upset but responsive. Saying little, being calm, simply being there: these were the things he needed, and these were not things it was difficult to give.

I have reached a point of irreversible certainty that I do not want to be with Max. Despite him seeming to be an honest man who is committed, and who is special and handsome. There are innumerable women for whom he can be this. I am not happy with him. This relationship didn't move at a kind or favourable pace, and I never got to make a real decision. Is it a coincidence that talk of suicide stopped once his father was in the ICU, once there was a new catastrophe? I can't say. I cannot say what he intends, or what another woman, with her own set of experiences, wouldn't feel trapped by.

Two nights ago, we had a drink at the bar across the street, and this night, just the talking without the cuddling or any of the benefits of being in our apartment, felt worse. A few times, as he talked, I teared up, which he read as empathy for his present situation, but in fact was out of lamentation for my own, because *what do I do*? I can't leave him now. We cannot just break up and still live together, and I certainly can't force him out. I don't actually want to give up my room, which I've had for over three years, the longest since my childhood home. The burial is Tuesday. I first said I wanted to go, out of a sense of duty, but this morning I went back on it and said I thought it was better, perhaps, only to attend the reception in the evening. He was upset. Less that I wouldn't be going than that I'd promised to and now wouldn't. Visibly very upset. And then, fuck, did I worry about everything. The fucking layers and layers of said-I-would that I've blanketed myself under because at the time it felt like a duty, or like the right thing to offer, or like the appropriate thing to do.

Walking across the street to our home, I finally shouted in frustration that I wanted to sob but couldn't, because I wasn't alone! I continued crying while we were in bed, with the lights off, when I faced away from him as he spoke. He brought up things I said I didn't want to do before the death, volunteering the prospects again: will you do this for a grieving man? I look at the way he behaves sometimes and think I really would not, even given the circumstances. But I don't know that! But, no: this is how Max is: the pushing, the not caring absolutely so much about what others prefer to do. It's just a natural application of this tendency to the present situation. And I know that this is *his* time, but it makes me feel awful that I don't even think he knows my parents' names. Sometimes I volunteer things from my own family life to provide him context for how I experience loss or attachment, and rather than ask me further how I feel, he just makes some flippant comment about how I should consider bringing it up to my therapist, because: have I looked into that? As if it's fucking possible that I hadn't! As if his basic expectation of me is that I am not studying these things, exploring them, writing about them every fucking day with extreme care.

* * *

On Friday after work, while Max was still at his mother's with his sister, I stopped by Maurice and Rebecca's, with whom I hadn't yet brought any of this up. And Maurice's mother came in, and even just listening to me matter-of-factly tell her the content of my day, she could hardly believe it all: well, I live with a partner now. It's very complicated. And his father just passed, yesterday. And I've just seen my own mother, who was married in Morocco two weeks ago. Oh, the last husband she moved away for? Well, that was years ago. The prospect of relocation isn't so complicated now because she's just been fired from her job. Well, it was a long time coming; she took this job in the throes of a deep depression... And her: "Oh, Catherine. You know you're always welcome here." (Which, I suppose, reminds me of whose death would make me flip my shit.)

* * *

Last night, I came home exhausted, unsure of when Max would return. I felt sad, tearful, trapped. Like I had no idea when this breakup could even happen. Like I have no idea how many more ways I'll display commitment while just trying to be good to the person who needs me right now. How I have nowhere to go, short of Maurice's house, to just sit in bed crying, because if Max were to get home and see me like this it would be so demonstrative, and I don't have the heart to tell him before the funeral that the tears aren't out of sympathy but out of a will to escape. And that any time I get close to hurting Max, I become suddenly aware of how fucking deep things are, how much he appears to believe in the certainty of this relationship. And suddenly I realize how mad he'll be at me for simply saying that I saw a future, for telling him I *would* be with him. But how couldn't I?! It just seemed like the thing to do to make the present bearable. It even seemed like a surprise to him when I described feeling like I was on a steady emotional decline since the day I flew back to Toronto. He suggested I go out because I appeared to be in such a bad mood last night, and I said, with whom? I reached out to Caroline, but she was busy. I had seen Maurice and Rebecca the evening prior. I asked: "Max, did you notice that I was out of Toronto for three months, and have since spent virtually every day with you? Who do you think I carry on a relationship with? Who do you think my friends are?" His suggestion was then that he should text Lori to ask her to include me in whatever her plans were, and I, of course: "What in the world are you thinking?!" Then he tries to get me to call him stupid, and I say, no, I'm not ever going to call you stupid, I'm not ever going to make you feel like your behaviour is the result of some permanent inability, considering this is exactly how you feel about yourself. This morning minor quibbles, too. Like, he goes, "I think a big fear of yours is that you're not emotionally equipped to handle things," and I go, "Yep! You got it!" and he goes, "See, even this response..." And I'm sure it's very odd that any of these conversations are taking place, considering his father died three days ago, but conversational time seems at once infinite and bound to old favourites.

It's almost as though my mother, stealthy, had done something so perversely smart and quietly caring to start rejecting, neglecting, and lashing out at me after her divorce from my father. Until a certain time, I was her confidante—a tiny source of care—but sometime in adolescence, this ended. Was it carelessness? Was it, as I'd always thought, just a reaction to me as an emblem of my father, whom she so resented? Or was it being so scarred by dominance and beholdenness that she wouldn't subject me to it—that she would never allow me, at a certain point, to be pressured into thinking she needed care? And did this involve stopping the faucet of extraneous care she could display to me, which I would otherwise feel the burden to repay?

I do not know how a better-equipped person deals with the pain of others, but knowing this is not my lot in life.

WHETHER THEY END IT OR I END IT, MY FINAL PLEAS ARE always the same: "I just like laughter and touch!"

It's true that not a dick is a lithium pill. You learn this when someone else's presence is so well normalized in your life that you can be completely despondent even when they're near.

* * *

Max's father's funeral is today, and I'm not going. Just dawdling around campus, smoking cigarettes in the sun. This is something that angers him. Rightfully in his perspective, I'm sure. Rightfully with the understanding that I want to be with Max, that I want each of our lives to be the life of the other. The information he is crucially missing is that I'm certain I don't want this.

I spend so much time in bed, so much time tearful. Guilty about what I cannot give, or what I won't. Guilty but with the knowledge that even in the wake of his father's death, his behaviour isn't exceptional. He will always see me as an extension of himself first, and a person of my own second. He has tricked himself into this, but I have helped him, without caution. It is both our faults.

I cannot imagine what it is to lose a father, because I'll never have to. Perhaps when I want to make my life with someone, I'll see it possible to imagine for them. Or perhaps even then I'll be unable. But we'll see.

This morning, leaving the house, I saw Freida leave hers. I called out to her, threw myself against her body in a move one would have to call a "hug," and immediately started crying. I felt bad for having trapped her. She did not ask to run into me. We simply live near each other. I am more eager to share my troubles with her than she is to share her own with me.

 Even during his experience of grief, Max feels bad that he cannot help when he sees that I have spent all day crying in bed with aches of head and body. His days haven't been the same, because they've been with his mother and sister, occupied. He thinks he cannot help me because of his duty to himself right now, or because of his duty to his family. This is not so. He cannot help because that is not how it works. He cannot help because only I can help myself, because I will not welcome intervention. I have never had helpful intervention. His will not be the first. Guilt and pressure where it regards him are chief among those things keeping me feeling sick. I'd be happier with a duty only to myself. I want autonomy. I want to be alone.

He wants me to be a better person for relationships, but I do not share this desire. He sees in me more that is curable than I want cured. What does he want? He tells me his peers advised, after his relationship with Cybil, that his next girlfriend should be his own age, but he took up with me even before that relationship was over. And they're right, perhaps. What do you think you're getting from some cute twenty-five-year-old with a will toward freedom who asks little from you and seems to desire to give you not much in return? You're getting exactly that. If you want someone with experience and confidence in providing a whole spectrum of care for others, be with them. He knows what I'm good for. Laughter and touch. Looking cute and saying cute things. If you want an older, serious woman: *find her*. She will be so glad to settle down. She will be so glad for an emotionally committed person. (She will likely have different expectations than I do. What they say about cakes.)

It is not necessary that either of us spend our lives like this, but when on earth is the right time to make this clear to him?

But it's absurd, though, right? That "privacy" just takes the root of privation and spins it to something quite good? I feel very sick, but I am smoking.

There's no mystery to being lovable. You have to demonstrate what looks like love according to whomever else's standard, or they have to trick themselves into thinking that, in some other circumstance, you'd be able to.

I think of the extreme verbal acuity that Max and I share as something that is a part of love, but I'm not being true to myself in thinking this. Hyperverbality is a characteristic of excitement. I want a love that gives me the comfort and security to shut the fuck up. I want a love that does not seek affirmation always. I want a love quiet at home making room for other things. I want a love that I don't worry about: neither losing nor maintaining it. I want us both occupied, quietly, working, reading the news. Laughing and touching. When the time is right. I want a love for which the laughter and touch just come forth from two lives being handled well, separately. Codependence is not desirable to me. To Max it is. Kindly, he's already warned me this week that I might think the worst has passed, but it hasn't. Grief lasts a very long time. He will never return to a state before the death. He will always be, from now on, in a post-death state.

* * *

People love others in relationships. Women especially, I think. It makes you socially valuable and socially monitorable. It makes you a link, a way of knowing another. It makes you less threatening. It makes your partner less threatening, too. The two of you form an observable unit keeping each other on an even keel, disturbing little. You're welcomed in a way you wouldn't otherwise be. You're cared for, because people will protect the loved ones of their friends. The more relationships, the more public familiality. It doesn't move too much and people trust it. To be in a relationship is to have someone vouch for you. It is a way of maintaining public regulation, and it is safe.

Terminology. When I last saw Caroline, she asked, as though it would be clarifying, "I know you love him, but are you in love with him?" *In*. Sure, yes, I'm in it every day. It's a struggle to get out of. But that doesn't mean I shouldn't try my best to.

Trying to make clear to Max how much less I feel I ask of him than he does of me, I ask, "What does it seem like I need from you?" And he answers, "Touch, lots of physical touch." So they do know some of how you feel, almost as if they've been eavesdropping. I can go without touch. I can handle myself.

* * *

I don't want Max in my future. He would know he felt the same way if he weren't so blinded by need right now. He knows I'm filling a need, and I know I'll decline to do so any longer starting next year. The worst *is* over. Even if he won't be "himself" for months or years, the worst that I'll feel myself beholden to is over. He mentioned even going to New York in January again. I expected he'd be more certain about his will to move if his father weren't here to care for any longer, and I was right. He asks in passing if I'll still want to be with him long-distance, and I say yes, in passing, too. But when we speak of this more seriously and with greater focus, I'll say no.

It's so funny, stupid, to think of staying "together" if he ends up spending months at a time in the US. For text messaging? So he would come home to someone guaranteed to fuck him? He'd just look to how checked out I seem and give himself permission to fuck someone else if he got the chance, and he'd leave me outright if someone nearer to him showed him care. I know these things. Just look at how he and I came to be. I shouldn't "be with him" while he is elsewhere so he has a semblance of security while he's actually, as he always is, open to better options. The time to pretend that my angel is innocent is over. He's an adult. We can be honest with each other. And we don't have to live our lives together, regardless of how unchallenging it is to cuddle.

He is a man who will rationalize whatever behaviour if he doesn't feel himself to be getting enough. And so we chose each other.

* * *

Big time for emotions. Feel settled today, as yesterday I sank incredibly low, weeping nude in a bathroom stall of the gym, thinking about: childhood; doom; attachment; grief; suffering; patience; and compassion for others and self. This was all slightly hungover following the previous day where, in the morning, I took a small amount of mushrooms and a medium dose of Dexedrine in order to write a paper, but instead was given the gift of extreme concentration to devote to dozens and dozens of advice columns, together with several articles on adult children of narcissists and/or adult children of alcoholics. Then, in the evening, coming down off speed slightly, I accompanied Max to a bar with his friends. It was delightful, a lovely time, a selection of people I really enjoy. Stayed late. We all stayed late enough that we were essentially escorted out by the staff at closing. Returning home, I fixed drinks for Max and myself with the last of some Siberian vodka that Ivan had brought back as a souvenir last winter. And then, drunk and on a comedown, I told Max I did not feel certain of continuing on with him. I said that I hoped he would move in January, that, returning to Toronto in September, I've always been certain he would have to. He asked, what if I stay? I said, in that case, I would leave the apartment. I told him that I didn't have any desire to take our lives and put them in a common direction. I told him that we need different things from people, and this incompatibility was too significant to bridge. I told him that even if I *could* change, he didn't make it so I wanted to. I said I thought of him as disloyal and I didn't trust him not to betray me the moment he feels mistreated. This is the only time he objected and said that my saying so hurt his feelings. I told him all I'd been thinking and he asked, "But it doesn't matter to you what we have?" I: "What do we have? Conversations. And if we weren't together, we'd have them with someone else." Ultimately after all this I gave him a long, tender, concerted blow job. We spent yesterday apart, but we talked a little after a show in bed, and this morning over breakfast I read him translations of Italian idioms involving food. Acknowledging everything that had happened the night before, we still spoke of travelling together to Italy someday.

* * *

Life has been consistent for a few days. I've been opened up to this relationship since I voiced my fears about it. I realized that what I was telling this man is that I'm too doomed not to move on from him because I'm built that way. But why move on? To what? To another I'd have to move on from, whom I wouldn't love like I love Max? Confessing that all actions feel like burdens can suddenly dispel those very burdens. Ate at his mother's and it felt like no particular thing this week, for instance. A great deal of my stress feels relieved. Surprise, surprise, the day I was on speed I had these *crystal-clear* revelations about life, which I didn't manage to articulate on paper, but they're still in my head, I'm sure. I think I've just accepted a whole lot of my life at once in a lovely way. Not worried about losing my life. Surprise, surprise! It's always your life! There's no decision you might otherwise have made!

I've chosen optimism: I'm not so doomed that I can't sustain intimacy. I've chosen to trust him, to trust that he won't abandon me once he's gotten what he needs. I've chosen that touch, love, and support can be the baseline of life from which everything else jumps forth, and love stops being difficult the moment you commit yourself to it. You say: the knowledge that I'm with him: that's where it starts. And it's a wonderful thing. I'm right: my life won't be what it was anymore. I've tried so hard to keep some semblance of my former life beneath the one I'm building with Max now, so that in case we split, I'll be able to return to it, but that won't happen. Even if we come apart, my life will come out the other side, changed.

* * *

What should I know already, goddamn? That I should trust my instincts, because they change less than they gather evidence.

* * *

After the time I told Max I didn't want to be with him, drunk and high on Dexedrine, I told him again, sober, and have since repeated it. It's difficult, as I feel extremely low and so am still affectionate with him. In light of this, he has called the whole thing "very silly." However, I am resolute. I'd prefer to eliminate the attachment to him from my life and repopulate that space with all that had once been there, even if at this time of the year what is there is stillness, darkness, and old TV shows I already know I like. He'll keep thinking it's impossible in the context of my attraction to him or my care for him, but this is how the lover interprets the beloved: everything is a ruse except love. Everything else is some conspiratorial charade. Everything else is something to *get to the bottom of.* But: no: I melt before touch, but I am certain I don't want it from him in my future. And now that I've made it clear to him, my feelings will not vacillate again.

There is a sort of eroticism I share with Max beyond anything I've had before. Freud has written that the sexual relation brings us back to a childlike place, and I've always thought of this as ridiculous. But now I see it. Near him, I hardly feel our bodies as separate, and I feel permitted to be at play with them. I am relaxed enough near him that my mind is free to roam in senseless and infantile ways, and I play it out with him physically. He does, too. I think he's better acquainted with his giddy unconscious. Being with him is to behave without a layer of conscious self-surveillance. Must be what happens when you spend so much time with someone that your mind hardly processes them as a separate being anymore. It would happen were I to share this—intimacy—with any number of people. It doesn't tell me that Max is right for me.

Last week, wrote Miles an email to ask if he'd like any company on NYE. He wrote back a very kind email to say that he's in a new relationship, one that would make this difficult. I wept a little. I had memories of how I felt with him over the summer: sometimes critical and never like we were matched optimally, but always very happy and always very free. When not together, never with the feeling that my life somehow bore upon him. It was quick, but, by God, it suited me well. I was never fucking worried about what something I said might incur—anger, a clumsiness in the kitchen handling knives that threatens to go awry. Miles and I could get annoyed with each other, but it never seemed *threatening*. It's not right to live in fear of what you might set off.

It is not selfish to do one's best to try to cultivate a life wherein there is the least resentment, the most engagement, the most stimulation, the most freedom, the most love. It's what one must do.

Update on life is there's been little of it, and I am waiting it out. Resistance is only a feeling until it's enacted, and it can't be enacted when you have little power to change things in your life. I don't feel a glimmer of love or affection any longer. I've spent some time lately *very* high, some time crying, some time sleeping. I've checked out of everything. Things are changing. I'll go days without the thought of possessing any power, and then I'll think about being alone again and having no one but myself to answer to, and then I'll feel seven feet tall and sturdy.

Last Saturday evening, I came home from Freida's incredibly, incredibly stoned. A pot high that felt like mushrooms. Edibles, smokables: a whole platter. When Max got in and shouted my name up the stairwell, I was *certain* I heard my father. I was terrified. I endure another self-pitying middle-aged man with anger management issues in whose presence I do not feel free. Another man who wants *company*, who couldn't care less about trying to understand me better, who hears what he wants.

This man, I can be stoned in front of, and I can cry in front of, and I can miss engagements in front of, and I can sleep eleven-hour nights in front of. At least I have those freedoms. I am, at least, allowed to feel blue.

* * *

It never turned into the sex I wanted, and they never turned into the conversations I wanted, and my fear of his anger still moderates my behaviour. Being loved is no mystery any longer. Find a delusional man who needs company to whom it doesn't matter if you feel sick. Do nothing in service of love, I've learned. Or: nothing in service of romantic love, and everything in service of: 1) fraternal/sororal love; 2) intellectual objects of love/fascination.

To be young: exactly when you might be at the height of your intellect, you're also struggling to make yourself up in a way you feel at peace with, and navigating relationships that perpetually offer you *firsts* to make sense of. So sensitive, but so eager. So ambitious but so soon to retreat in fear. Learning what can be changed and what must be accepted. Figuring out which opportunities have been lost and what is still possible. Figuring out who you're responsible to, or how simple that responsibility can be. Figuring out: no one to whom you don't consent. I don't need anyone's surveillance, and I don't need anyone's love.

* * *

I've finished a fall semester that was abysmal but not as abysmal as last year's, and I've been through many mood swings. Today, I became suddenly aware of the smell of spice coming out of a restaurant, and I felt my senses come back.

* * *

It's difficult to understand how Max endures my pessimism. For a moment. Until I remember that pessimism and distrust can work the same as absence: Max can always imagine how good things might be if I were only around for him as I have been during moments he's idealized.

Max's love: I'll never feel it. If I feel it for a moment, I'll take the first opportunity to stop. I've seen myself recently carrying out a stereotypical exercise in feminine masochism: refuse to express to your partner something important to you, and then, after he's failed to do it, resent him. Retreat instead. Tell yourself that the clumsy man will always fail you because everyone fails you. I am the only person who fails myself in a way that I can anticipate and consent to.

Ivan says it's the fashion in his graduate cohort for people to carry on labour-unintensive long-distance relationships, requiring under an hour upkeep per day, reassurance via a text-message check-in, and that these tend to be conducive to academic survival. So the next step in my relationship with Max could actually turn out to be less decimating to me than the first—instead a lucky little pick-me-up during a time of the year that I don't tend to be very sexually hungry, anyway.

Max's favourite experience of me is neither when he's confused nor when I'm unusually stimulated. It's when we're out together for averagely nice nights. It's when we eat together in the morning, listen to something, banter absentmindedly about not much. Moments during which we are not glowing but instead our sustainably average selves. I am almost pathologically unwilling to extend more than average effort toward him, lest I feel used later. So he doesn't actually love any fantasy. He just loves me, daily, naturally, nude or clothed, quick or slow.

When I see him clumsy or slow, I tell myself I don't love him, or that I shouldn't. I should love a more organized or better disciplined person. I should love someone I haven't met, who doesn't exist. I shouldn't love someone who, whenever I express sadness or anger with him, is immediately concerned, and tells me how sorry he is, and that he wishes he knew better how to give me what I want, or who wishes I told him more readily what it *is* that I want. No! I should love instead the fantasy of some absent person, or I should love someone who isn't responsible to me, or I should love something I can't see who keeps me awake just as hunger does. Nothing in service of itself: everything in service of some other thing. Everything threaded with distrust because I can't make the decision to settle down and have faith in this person who vows himself to me, because I'm too anxious of the threat that he'll leave me, and it will all have been for naught. How can I know that I don't love Max when I've never known love before? All I've known has been the feeling of hunger for people who evoked nothing but it. Hunger that made me live desperately and fast. Of course love, in its active presence, would have to be slowing. You don't have to spring forth quickly to claim something that's yours.

Thought both communistic and pessimistic: just as nothing is anyone's, nothing is mine. (As soon as I believe in assignment and belonging, I might have to believe that I have something, too.)

It may sometimes be others, but it is always me. You will never make yourself worse off by learning how to accept and express love safely, and how to cooperate, how to stake space for your own life while sharing it with the life of another. I will not have given something up—I will have gotten better. Look to who is willing to be optimistic. Do you love them? Even if it's a comfortable and domestic love rather than an overpowering one, do it with them.

I sometimes think, in patronization, that Max should get over me and love someone fawning and insecure who seeks to mimic him, or to transform herself into something more resembling him to win his affection. Like certain men are used to. I think I'll never make him happy: that will. But I don't know better than Max does what will make him happy. He tells me ongoing: I do. Not the promise or imagination of me: me. And he makes me happy, too, when I let him. Only willing, I can have more love and everything else, too.

You can say yes to something besides the void. You can say yes to someone you know, though never completely. You can say yes to someone who says yes to you. Audibly, decipherably, consistently. You can say yes without being forced, upon your own decision. You can say yes with an optimism that helps to trick you into the idea that it's easy.

* * *

I try my best to stay positive, but I may have to wait for the next opportunity.

Being wanted is worse than being unwanted. It's taken me too many years to learn this.

* * *

What else. For the year. Resolutions. Oh, I don't know. Stick to a schedule. Keep up with readings. Establish a good rapport with my professors. Express myself more simply. Exercise, as I love, five times a week. Visit my grandparents, who love me and little else, once a week, if I can. Mom, too, although she will likely have a job and is satisfied by text messages. Try to make sure you're at Maurice and Rebecca's, playing cards once a week, too. Maintain your most stimulating correspondences. Go dancing at least once every couple of weeks. Maintain friendships with Ruby, Caroline, and Freida—do this with them. Eat more nutritiously and with greater regularity; prepare meals. Spend more time on friendships that are collaborative or form around common interests. Know that perhaps you are past the time in your life in which every new friendship has to be an intimate one. Spend late nights at the library; feel the thrill of research; aim for clarity; know that it is possible.

Sludge

It may be wired into me to be turned on by the promise of a threat to order—a way of commingling failed heteronormative fears of abandonment and a real longing for change, or a longing to cultivate public change through the nex(us)(es) of my own relationships. Allergy to care can take much the same form as resistance to tradition. So stupid: as traditional and closed as my pairing with Max feels, one thing I like about it is that it's somewhat *public*—Max and I both work publicly with words (or, God, desire to). There's something generous and generative about this, as though regardless of who we're fucking, we still produce something from the pairing to put forth into the world.

Because, here's this: as much as fucking isn't revolutionary, writing isn't either? Even writing with subversive elements? Everything fits. That's the fear. Everything participates in the economy that permits it.

It's possible that the only way to live free of immediate constraint from the economy you'd prefer not to consent to is being a criminal in a community of criminals or to inherit a bunch of private capital. There's compliance, criminality, and private capital! (And love, gifts, community—but everything given must originate *somewhere*.)

I just want to desire—and be gratified by my desire for—something both politically progressive and pragmatic. And I would like the desire of others near me to fall in line with my own. I want it to cooperate with school and work. I want to live cultivating an interpersonal ethic that works to change larger public ethics. I want a psyche that has sucked in so much garbage from outside to project itself back out, cleansed, onto the heart of the world, *eliminating capitalism.* Is that too much to ask?

* * *

I'm in Toronto, Max is in New York, we have broken up, and I feel calm and strength as I return to my life. Phewf.

I don't care about being lovable. I'd prefer to be strong, focused, self-sufficient, and perhaps a bit unruly, too. Onward, forward, to being alone, and to otherwise being only with people I *crave.* I can't wait to start fucking again. I get to fuck again! I get to fuck and then only continue on fucking those who don't interrupt me while I'm talking! And then those people will leave my house! They will leave my house after we've really *fucked* each other! All the world will be new again!

* * *

I find it difficult to elevate my mood or energy levels, but also to read *Mind Over Mood* without laughing. "In the past, my heartrate returned to normal when I [...] thought in non-catastrophic ways."

On all my most optimistic days, I try to come to abstract notions of what's right and good, but it's hard to bring about a climax from this. What good masturbatory material is made of light? My orgasms have come only from darkness. They have not come from the playfulness of the sexual encounters that have made me feel most utopian. Did Max, who made me feel slow, dark, and tired, help me to foster a mind of erotic material that was for the first time potent on its own? He slowed me to the deep, dark sludge. I don't *like* what I come to. I needn't. There's always shame, envy, dominance. Not quite prosocial. Will I move toward a life where I come to something that looks like the sex I have, or that I want to have, or that I think I want to have? I love a sexual encounter that feels friendly and fun because it suits my values, but I never masturbate to "friendly and fun." I masturbate to things getting very uncomfortable. I want to like the sex I desire in my utopian mind, but I come instead to the sludge.

I can come to what I think is a bit gross—or to anything besides perfectly equal division of touch—in private or with company. What makes me come can be the underside of things. What makes me come does not have to be my intellectual favourite. It can be the reverse of what I want to see in the world. It betrays an idea of ethical consistency: I want to come to what is good and light because I want to *be* good and light. What a joke. Who could expect the achievement of sexual satisfaction without being able to come to terms with the reality of their own character.

If soon I stop feeling so dark, will my sexual imaginary move with me to match this? Is it just a lack of concordance of mind and intention? Who do I really trust so much to practise something utopian with? Maybe shame is what I feel, so I like the fantasies that make use of it. Let sex bring you into the gloom of your psyche, just like in your masturbation fantasies. Maybe then there will be concordance. Maybe then there will be orgasms. And maybe then I'll be past the childish idea of some abstract future where sexual desire should relate coherently to considered intent or political will. That my desire should coherently relate to *ethical fucking purity*.

* * *

Adam Phillips writes, "Our utopias tell us more about our lived lives and privations than about our wished-for lives." If I read about a hypothetical program for life all mapped out, I see it less for what it will produce than for what it details that I recognize I do not have. I see it sketch out what I'm missing. More importantly, I see it sketch out what I'm missing regardless of whether or not it's something I want.

Sources

Agamben, Giorgio, *The Highest Poverty: Monastic Rules and Form-of-life.* Translated by Adam Kotsko. Stanford: Stanford UP, 2013.

Badiou, Alain. *Saint Paul: La fondation de l'universalisme.* Paris: Presses Universitaires de France, 1997.

Barthes, Roland. *A Lover's Discourse: Fragments.* Translated by Richard Howard. New York: Hill and Wang, 2010.

—— *How to Live Together: Novelistic Simulations of Some Everyday Spaces.* Translated by Kate Briggs. New York: Columbia UP, 2013.

—— *Sade Fourier Loyola.* Paris: Éditions du Seuil, 1971.

Beckett, Samuel. *Worstward Ho.* New York: Grove Press, 1983.

Branden, Nathaniel. "Isn't Everyone Selfish?" In *The Virtue of Selfishness: A New Concept of Egoism.* Edited by Ayn Rand. New York: New American Library, 1964.

Deleuze, Gilles, and Félix Guattari. *Anti-Oedipus: Capitalism and Schizophrenia.* Translated by Robert Hurley, Mark Seem, and Helen R. Lane. New York: Viking Press, 1977.

Freud, Sigmund. *Dora: An Analysis of a Case of Hysteria.* New York: Simon & Schuster, 1997.

Greenberger, Dennis, and Christine A. Padesky. *Mind Over Mood: Change How You Feel by Changing the Way You Think.* New York: Guilford Press, 1995.

Invisible Committee, The. *To Our Friends.* Translated by Robert Hurley. South Pasadena: Semiotext(e), 2015.

Kierkegaard, Søren. *Either/Or.* Translated by Howard V. Hong and Edna H. Hong. Princeton, N.J.: Princeton UP, 1987.

Millet, Catherine. *Jealousy.* Translated by Helen Stevenson. London: Serpent's Tail, 2009.

Nancy, Jean-Luc. *Corpus.* Translated by Richard A. Rand. New York: Fordham UP, 2008.

—— *Noli me tangere: On the Raising of the Body.* Translated by Sarah Clift, Pascale-Anne Brault, and Michael Naas. New York: Fordham UP, 2008.

Negri, Antonio. *Spinoza for Our Time: Politics and Postmodernity.* Translated by William McCuaig. New York: Columbia UP, 2013.

Phillips, Adam. "Against Self-Criticism," *London Review of Books* 37, no. 5 (2015): 13-16.

—— *Missing Out: In Praise of the Unlived Life.* London: Hamish Hamilton, 2012.

Rancière, Jacques. *The Ignorant Schoolmaster: Five Lessons in Intellectual Emancipation.* Translated by Kristin Ross. Stanford: Stanford UP, 1991.

Schultz, Kathryn. "The Really Big One," *New Yorker*, July 2015.

Svenonius, Ian. *Supernatural Strategies for Making a Rock 'n' Roll Group.* New York: Akashic Books, 2013.

Tiqqun. *Preliminary Materials for a Theory of the Young-Girl.* Translated by Ariana Reines. Cambridge: Semiotext(e), 2012.

Weil, Simone. *Gravity and Grace.* Translated by Emma Craufurd. London; New York: Routledge, 1987.

Acknowledgements

Thank you to Alex, Amelia, Claire, Daniel, and Rachel for being the sources of stability, curiosity, and joy that anchor me in the world. Thank you to Derek and Jacob for reading my earliest drafts, and to Malcolm for his skilful editing, without which those drafts would not have been made into something more. For their friendship and creative support, I am leaving out dozens. Thanks, everyone.

Catherine Fatima is a writer who was born, raised, and currently lives in Toronto. *Sludge Utopia* is her first book.

Colophon

Distributed in Canada by the Literary Press Group:
www.lpg.ca

Distributed in the United States by Small Press Distribution:
www.spdbooks.org

Shop online at www.bookthug.ca

Designed by Malcolm Sutton
Edited for the press by Malcolm Sutton
Copy-edited by Stuart Ross

BOOK
PRODUCTION
WAR ECONOMY
STANDARD